THE TIN-PAN MAN

THE TIN-PAN MAN

P. A. BECHKO

SAGEBRUSH
Large Print Westerns

First published in Great Britain by ISIS Publishing Ltd
First published in the United States by Five Star

Published in Large Print 2012 by ISIS Publishing Ltd.,
7 Centremead, Osney Mead, Oxford OX2 0ES
by arrangement with
Golden West Literary Agency

British Library Cataloguing in Publication Data
Bechko, P. A.
    The tin-pan man.
    1. Western stories.
    2. Large type books.
    I. Title
    813.5'4–dc23

ISBN 978–0–7531–8984–9 (pb)

Printed and bound in Great Britain by
T. J. International Ltd., Padstow, Cornwall

Dedicated with much love and gratitude to my mother, Betty, whose support and encouragement has, more often than she knew, given me the strength to press on

CHAPTER
ONE

It was a black night with barely a sliver of a moon to light the way. Samantha Cameron had been in the saddle for hours, wandering in circles. She jerked angrily at the wadded-up fabric of her skirts, trying to adjust it more comfortably between herself and the saddle leather. In a way, the situation had made her feel like a kid again. Back then she would steal off to the stables in her little girl dresses to sneak out one of the horses — her favorite, Marabella — to go riding like a hellion across the Virginia hills. To the horror of her conventional mother, she had been seen by every neighbor within miles, her skirts flapping wildly in the wind created by her passing, hair streaming from its pins, pantaloon-clad legs pressed tightly to Marabella's withers. Now, if she had not been so exhausted, so desperate, and so terrified, the remembered image would have brought a smile to her lips, despite all that the years had handed her since that time.

The palms of her small hands began sweating against the reins as she remembered sneaking this horse out of the stable. It had been hours since Samantha had executed her escape from the town of Saquarra, and she was damned well off for being shut of it. It was no more than a nest of outlaws. A town willingly handed over to scum by a pack of upstanding citizens who had treated her like a leper. And all because she had had the misfortune of being dragged there against her will and sold to Mississippi Pike while on her way to accept a new teaching position in Prescott, Arizona.

She tugged at her skirts again, wishing that there had been time to do more than slip from her room, catch up the horse, and ride for all she was worth away from that miserable town. The layered skirts were cumbersome, and she had brought along but few supplies. There was the canteen, half filled with water and now looped over the saddle horn, and the rifle in the scabbard alongside her knee.

The mare's hoofs clicked against stone, and Samantha squinted pale blue eyes against the darkness in an attempt to see what lay ahead and offer the animal some guidance. She stroked the mare's neck as the game little horse strode out — long, slender legs moving like they could carry her clear to California without stopping.

"You're a lot like my Marabella was," Samantha said to her mount. "Beautiful and strong."

The horse snorted and kept walking.

"I hope we're not going in circles. If we were, though, we'd still see the lights of Saquarra. I don't care where we're headed, as long as it's away from there."

The mare beneath her tossed her head, bit jangling.

"Shhh. We have to be very quiet. This is Apache country."

2

As if understanding her words, the mare quieted, lifting her gait to a jog. Samantha did not check her pace. They needed to put miles between themselves and Saquarra. If Mississippi Pike sobered up fast enough, he would be coming after her. That thought was horrifying to Samantha, sending chills along her spine colder than the desert night. She allowed the little horse to move even more swiftly.

They skirted a low hill, scrub and cactus alternately tearing at the hem of her flapping skirts. Suddenly, right before her, even blacker than the darkness of the night, an empty pit yawned directly in front of her. There wasn't time to turn or stop, and in an instant it would swallow them both.

There was no way to save the mare, although Samantha reflexively jerked back on the reins before throwing herself clear of the horse. At the same moment the mare stepped out into the open space before her. Samantha hit the ground with a thud, her head bouncing off the ground, the wind knocked out of her. It was then she heard the terrified squeal of the mare who had continued tumbling forward into the ravine. Samantha held her breath. There had been no footing for the horse to regain, just the air beneath its feet as the earth opened up in a perpendicular drop. Years, hundreds of them, had conspired with wind and rain to carve this chasm out of the desert floor. A path for the water to flow became a death trap for the valiant mare. Through the darkness it plummeted.

The mare's landing was not as fortuitous as had been Samantha's. There was a horrible cracking sound, like

3

green wood splintering, then a shrill cry and the heavy thump of horse connecting with sand. The effect of the fall was audible to Samantha at the top of the ravine.

Ignoring the tenderness in her body as she shifted her weight, she was instantly on her feet, reeling unsteadily down the sandy slope of the ravine wall in the dark toward the animal, sprawled at the bottom. Tears slid down Samantha's face as she tumbled down and down, the sand and dirt swirling about her, spraying into her eyes and mouth, mixing with her tears. Finally she was at the bottom, where the night's darkness seemed even blacker as she strained eyes and ears to locate the mare. She stumbled ahead, following the uneven gasps of breathing coming from the mare as her eyes slowly adjusted to the dense darkness. She found the horse.

"Shhhh," Samantha offered by way of consolation as she dropped beside the mare and tried to calm her thrashings. "Take it easy, girl. Don't try to stand. We'll have to take it slow. We'll have to be more careful. We shouldn't have been moving so fast in the darkness. Just lie quiet a minute. Easy, girl . . . you'll be all right." The soft tones of her voice seemed to have a soothing effect on the horse. Never mind the rising fear that she was lying to the beast. Never mind the horrible clenching in her chest which told her it wasn't all right at all.

"Come on now, we're partners. We'll rest just a few minutes, then we'll have to push on. Pike would probably be as mad at you as he would at me if he catches us, and he's not someone you want mad at you."

4

Holding the mare securely around the neck, the touch of her hand and her soft words kept the animal down on her side, legs outstretched, her breath coming in harsh pulls. Samantha continued to comfort her while trying to determine the extent of the injury. It was touch, not sight, that made things clear. The horse's right shank was bent sharply at an odd angle. It was broken badly.

"Oh, God!" Samantha stroked the animal as tears streamed down her dusty cheeks. She started to shake uncontrollably. "Oh, God, I'm sorry. I'm so sorry."

Samantha knew what she had to do. She could not allow the animal who had come to mean so much to her in so short a time to suffer. With a trembling hand she pulled the rifle free of the scabbard. How she hated guns — ever since the war. She hated the touch of them, the sound of them, the effect of them. Yet she knew, like now, they served a purpose. She looked at the outline of the mare in the dark, her own breathing strained. The poor animal. She must not lose her nerve. Tears flowing, throat seized to the point of closing, she stood up, leveled the rifle at the mare's beautiful head, and pulled the trigger.

The resounding crack of the shot covered Samantha's simultaneous wail of grief. She allowed the rifle barrel to drop, gunsmoke curling into the folds of her skirts. The mare was out of her misery. Samantha knew that there was no such simple solution to her own plight.

She stroked the mare's head one last time, then collected the rifle and the canteen, and started off down the wash, sinking in the loose sand with each stride.

She had to move even faster now. The gunshot could have been heard for miles — by Apaches or by Mississippi Pike.

Sand collected uncomfortably in her ankle-high, lace-up boots, and dust filmed even more heavily her finely-boned face. The grit served to conceal the darkening bruise on her jaw which she had received in the leap from the mare. Samantha, staggering from exhaustion, barely managed to keep to her feet but stumbled on. The sun had appeared in the sky some time before, though she wasn't exactly sure when it had happened or how enough time could have passed to make it possible. Her rifle was gone now. Sometime during the long hours of the night she had fallen, and it had been flung off into the darkness. She had not been able to gather her wits enough to search for it, although, when she had stumbled across the steep, rock-strewn path leading up out of the wash, she had taken it without any consideration at all. It had been automatic then. One foot in front of the other she had stomped determinedly up out of the arroyo which had cost her so much. But between then and now she had become blurry-brained.

Direction was chosen by putting the sun at her back, where it pounded mercilessly. The heat worked its way through the fibers of her dress. She didn't dare think about what she would do once the sun moved across the heavens to shine in her eyes. There was no thought spared either for the canteen, now empty save for a swallow or two of warm, metallic-tasting water.

"It wasn't supposed to be like this," she groaned to the desert scrub she passed. "I should be somewhere by now."

She lurched forward, caught the hem of her skirts beneath her foot, and careened into a large boulder, catching herself on its rough surface before she could fall to the ground. Face reddened by sun and effort, Samantha at last stopped where she was, massaged her scraped hand, and sat down on the rock.

"Just for a little while," she mumbled to herself. "I'll just rest here till I can catch my breath. Then I'll head for Tucson or Tombstone. It won't be long now."

She turned back the cuffs and pinched open the top couple of buttons of her high-necked dress. A lot more of the day lay ahead of her than what she had already put behind. A rest would do her good. She couldn't get where she was going if she collapsed from exhaustion.

Time expanded and contracted in strange, unpredictable ways, so that Samantha had no idea how long she had been sitting on the rock. In fact, she had been in such a stupor she was hardly aware of time passing at all. That was until she felt a strange weight against her boot. Something rubbing, pressing against her foot. A dry, rasping sound accompanied the undulating pressure. She nearly jumped to her feet but checked the impulse, managing instead to rise in a slow, smooth motion, freezing where she stood when an ominous rattle came from beneath her skirts.

Samantha's flesh rippled in response to that sound. She waited. It was quiet. She tried to convince herself it was not what she feared. She poised herself and prepared to take a tiny step. Again the rattle. Clearer. More insistent. Again she felt something brush up against the leather of her boots. Still as stone Samantha drew a shuddering breath and clenched her fists at her sides, staring down at the hem of her gingham skirts, hanging straight and full in the dead calm of morning heat.

She wanted to scream, but the emerging sound was only a dry whisper in the silent air. "Holy Mother of God, there's a snake under me!"

CHAPTER
TWO

A wheel of the wagon bumped over a large rock, setting the wares of the peddler's wagon clanging and banging against each other. A puff of dust rose from beneath the wheel to hang suspended on the breathless desert air. Tumbleweeds lay scattered across the open stretch, becalmed in the arid heat. The sun blazed unchecked by clouds or trees, sucking the juices out of any living thing fool enough to be traveling with the sun at its zenith.

The wagon limped and creaked its way across the cracked and burning earth while the single horse drawing it trudged wearily along, not truly exhausted, since he was a prime piece of horseflesh in top condition, but plainly thoroughly tired of it all. Heat rose in undulating waves off the desert floor, and the clang-banging of the peddler's pots and pans kept brassy and annoying rhythm with the sluggardly pace for long minutes after the offending rock had set the noisy wares in motion.

Zachariah Kane sat hunched on the driver's box, dun-colored hatbrim pulled low to block dust and glare. A thick black beard, ratty and bristling, fringed his hard, square jaw. His eyes, protected at least partly by the brim of his slouch hat, were red-rimmed, stinging and scratchy, continually tearing before the onslaught of airborne grit, and shaded by heavy brows hitched together in a thoughtful expression. Wary as a once-creased grizzly, Kane took stock as the wagon rolled slowly forward. He was alone. One man crossing the face of a most inhospitable wilderness. A desert wilderness that was bound to collect its due. Nevertheless, he was confident that it would not collect from him. In the passing years he had criss-crossed the barren expanse many times over. And, in the course of that time, he had traded with the Indians, fought them, and run from them. He had kept his powder dry, his tobacco handy, and he was still alive — a condition many others who had attempted to travel the vast expanses no longer enjoyed.

Momentarily Kane dropped his gaze to his hands, as darkly browned by the sun as the parched hills rolling up out of the broad basin, north of the wagon's course. When he looked forward again, he saw a sight that puzzled him more than the clattering pots and pans in the wagon irritated him. Up ahead, shrouded in a veil of dust, a lone figure stood on the open desert. Kane could make out nothing more at this distance. Turning it over slowly in his mind, Kane gave thought to the situation, trying to decide whether he should detour around the odd individual. Such decisions were not to be made lightly. This was rough country, and he was an experienced man. Three years, fighting in the war between the States, had hardened him, taught him lessons no nineteen-year-old should have had to learn, but he nonetheless carried them with him. Finally, he settled on just letting his horse plod forward at the same pace, at least until he could get a better look at how things stood.

He shifted his measuring gaze away from the lone figure to the hillcrests surrounding him on all sides. War training. Look for the enemy where you don't see him. The high ground was empty. But, by now, every Apache within miles knew exactly where he was and would be deciding whether he was worth the trouble or not. For the most part the Apaches judged him too crazy to mess with. Those who didn't knew his wagon and were more interested in trading for knives, cards of needles, buttons, and feathered finery for their women. If they decided to kill him, their source would be gone and that would be mighty hard to explain to the womenfolk, especially since some of his iron kettles had become prized possessions among them.

Kane toted everything from snake oil to cloth and needles in the back of his wagon. As he well knew, there could be no more welcome visitor at an outlying settlement or ranch than a peddler, even though he himself much preferred his hermit's life to the times of necessary mixing with people. He also preferred not to announce his presence too loudly. He glanced irritably over his shoulder because he still had not become accustomed to the sound of the clatter of his wares, and he doubted that he ever would. Barring wind or a serious hole or rock, blessed quiet would be his companion for the approaching encounter.

Inexorably his wagon ate away at the gap separating him from the lone figure, rooted motionlessly to the baked earth. He shifted the reins to his left hand, reached beneath the wagon seat with his right for his Winchester, and propped it beside him. Tin pans and skillets had quieted where they hung from hooks in the roof of the wooden wagon, swinging in tandem as the horse in the traces before him plodded on. Kane watched more closely for over-size rocks.

As his wagon sluiced its way through the sand, nearing the solitary figure, it became unsettlingly clear he was approaching a woman. A small shudder skipped up his spine. He liked women as much as the next man, but they made him nervous in ways even more pronounced than the effect a beautiful woman, under the right circumstances, had on his desire. Worse than that — much worse — he was convinced they had a way of getting caught in the crossfire if a situation were dangerous. And this situation, if not dangerous, was uncommon to say the least.

Samantha had been trying to decide whether her current position was worse than the one she'd left in Saquarra, when she heard the wagon's approach and then caught sight of it out of the corner of her eye. Her first thought was how to signal the wagon's driver since she dare not move. Then, she realized, there was no need. The slowly approaching wagon seemed to be heading directly for her. Even though her predicament would not be immediately obvious to the driver of that wagon, the fact that she was out here, alone in the middle of nowhere, must attract his attention without any prompting on her part. She had held herself

12

motionless this long; she could wait a little longer. Her hair gleamed white-blonde in the sun. A sudden breath of soft, warm air twirled it across her sun-burned face, but she did not lift a hand to push it aside. A long, careful sigh oozed from between dry, cracked lips.

Ordinarily she was a practical and tough-minded woman. Her past before being brought to Saquarra seemed ancient history; the time since then a blur of humiliating events, and then the pass that had brought her here — and here was more than a little unnerving. She focused pale blue eyes downward, once more attempting to see past the curve of her full skirts to the ground. Nothing. But it was still there. She had learned early in life about unkind twists and turns, but this irony was something entirely new.

The long night past was nothing short of a nightmare, leaving her at its end alone with nothing, baking here in the sun's blistering glare. She might have done something about her predicament had it not been for that damned snake. She hated snakes. She was sweating in her effort to remain still, fear sending a rippling shudder through her body. Her breath caught in her dry throat because of it. A softly grating slither glided across one short, laced boot as the loathsome creature rearranged itself. There wasn't room enough for the two of them beneath the bell of her skirts. She wished the wagon would hurry.

The peddler's wagon crunched to a halt near the woman. Zachariah Kane leaned out a bit from the driver's box uncertain at her lack of response to his arrival. She was of slight form and slender proportions — still as a statue, not even turning her head in acknowledgment of him. He noticed the sleeves of her blue and white checked dress were unbuttoned and rolled back, the lace-trimmed neck open to a daring *décolletage* where perspiration trickled in a moist trail from her chin. It was easy to understand the need to remain cool, but it was an old mistake that many unfamiliar with the desert's ways made. Soon she would be suffering for it. Her exposed skin was already burned to a bright, glowing red, and, where sweat wasn't trickling, it covered her skin in a shimmering sheen. Just like frying fat in a skillet.

A good-size boulder was beside her, and a gentle breeze gusted and died, stirring her skirts only a little. She was disheveled, plainly exhausted, but unmoving. It was perplexing. While Kane was keenly aware that it could be a trick of some bandits to trap the unwary, he could see nothing stirring for miles. He was neither unwary nor possessed by that marked lack of good sense that a large number of settlers heading west out of Independence displayed with alarming regularity.

His rifle was close at hand, and he surveyed the scene with close scrutiny. She was definitely alone. There was no cover within miles of this place where a man could conceal himself in ambush. Still, the woman had not moved since he had pulled up beside her. He was beginning to wonder if she was touched. Maybe she had been out in the desert sun without a hat for too long.

14

"Ma'am," Kane began tentatively from the seat of his wagon, the reins held loosely in his left hand, his right near his rifle, "looks like you could use a ride."

Damn' right I could, Samantha thought indignantly. *You fool, get down off that cursed wagon and give me a hand!* Her throat was so parched, there wasn't much left of her voice, but she tried, her breath barely carrying the name of her source of distress.

Kane did not get a direct answer to his observation, but he was aware of her lips moving and a soft, shushing sound issuing from them like she was trying to warn him to silence. He had not intended to climb down from the wagon box. Yet the woman *was* alone. What the hell else could he do? He was cautious and took his rifle with him when he jumped down.

Again the soft sound emitting from her lips. "Sssssnaaaa . . ."

When he came up alongside her, he was wondering what he was going to do with her if she was touched. Then, for the first time, he understood what she was saying to him in that low, dry whisper.

"Sssssnake . . ."

Kane's glittering eyes flicked from the stiff, still woman to the hard-baked ground at her feet. At first he saw nothing — and her sanity was about to become suspect again — when he recognized the shape and dusty coloring of a desert sidewinder almost completely concealed by the hem of her full skirts. Unable to stand the heat of the direct sun, the snake had somehow managed to find shelter in the combined shade of her skirts and the large rock beside her. The sun had moved since, leaving only the haven of her skirts. A dun-colored curve of the snake was all that was visible, but from it alone Kane could tell it had to be a mighty big one.

Hers was an intriguing dilemma he had never come across before. Extricating herself, had he not come along, would have provided her quite a challenge. For a moment he just stared at the serpent, wondering how it could have gotten where it had without her being aware of its approach.

"Please," again the voice, still dry, but a little louder now, "hurry."

"Hang on."

He disappeared from Samantha's view, reappearing within a few moments with a long pole in hand.

Eyes wide with apprehension she watched uneasily as the strange, unkempt man swung the pole before him. She had preferred the sight of the rifle, though in her position she did not have much to say about anything. His intent was plain. He was going to tease that damned snake out from under her skirts. She watched in fearful fascination as he used the tip of the slender pole to push gently at the hem of her skirts which covered the larger portion of the snake. Instantly the snake took offense at the change in its habitat, whipping itself into a threatening coil.

Giving a low whistle of appreciation at the size of the beast, Kane saw the rigid woman go ashen beneath the brilliant red of her sunburn — as if his whistle had put her in mortal danger. Another one caught in the crossfire, as far as he was concerned. However she had

16

come to be out here alone, he decided he was going to have to rescue her fast and get shut of her in the nearest town. He would not be responsible for her. For now, she was out of danger, as he had become the center of the snake's anger. The rattles buzzed, and the snake swayed menacingly in mid-air, poised to strike.

"I've got his attention now, ma'am."

Samantha gingerly lifted her skirts. "Shoo!"

A breath of air stirred the cloth, caressing the snake's back. It swayed, as if considering which direction to turn.

Kane swore softly under his breath, then, tapping and poking, he teased the snake back toward him until it struck at the pole he held. The shock of the impact jarred his arm to his shoulder, surprising him with the strength behind it. The snake gathered itself higher, extending the reach of its strike, shook its rattles furiously, and swayed with the movement of the pole, until the air was alive with the sound. Those glistening, beady eyes were fixed beyond the length of wood, glaring at Kane. The sidewinder's movements were not centered now so much on striking the pole as at striking beyond it, around it, reaching the true tormentor. Its tongue flicked nervously as the snake swayed.

He waved the pole in front of the creature, then made a quick jabbing motion. With a lightning strike that caught the wood about midway up its length, the rattler retaliated. Another jolt. With no hesitation the snake recoiled, again facing the man but reluctant to give up its shelter beneath the lady's skirts. Kane grinned. Damned if that snake didn't know who the

17

real enemy was. Not the pole that was continually thrust before it, but instead the man who wielded it.

"Would you please just kill it!" Again that softly feminine voice — dry, rasping, with a note of pleading, coloring the tone.

"Not just yet, ma'am."

Silence.

Kane was beginning to sweat. If he allowed his concentration to waver, he might well be the recipient of a full load of the snake's venom — or at least as much as the critter had left after hitting that pole. While the poison of the sidewinder was not generally believed to be as potent as that of some of its closer relatives, and although it was plainly diminished in volume, Kane did not care to find out first hand.

Slowly, harassing the rattler into striking and recoiling, he drew it out into the full sunlight. Once there, the battle was won. The snake's sensitivity to heat made it unable to tolerate the combined sear of the burning sand and the blazing afternoon sun for long. For the snake retreat was salvation.

Exposed, the sidewinder almost at once displayed intolerance of this new environment. It appeared to blink in the full exposure of the sun's brilliance. Soon exhaustion would take over, and, if the snake was not within reach of some shady rock, he would never have the opportunity to doze beneath a lady's skirts again. Cursed with the inability to regulate its body temperature, even more so than other snakes, a sidewinder would perish quickly beneath the scorching sun.

The varmint seemed to give Kane a parting glare before sliding off across the sand, using its odd, sideways, whip-like motion to carry it along in swift retreat.

Samantha sank down in the warm sand. She felt a bit giddy from her long ordeal. Black dots danced before her eyes. She was grateful to the stranger, but unbalanced. Her red-rimmed eyes were fixed on him from beneath puffy lids.

"Are you crazy? God! Why didn't you just shoot it?"

"I never shoot a man unless he's trying to kill me . . . or a beast unless I'm hungry. Now, if you're hungry . . . ?" He half turned to follow the deposed snake.

Samantha grimaced.

With a knowing smile Kane took her arm and lifted her gently to her feet. "You better get out of the sun. You already look about half fried."

She sighed. "I'm sorry. I really do appreciate what you just did. It's just that I've been standing out here for quite a while."

He guided her to the back of the wagon. "What's your name?"

"I'm Samantha . . . Samantha Cameron. I came from a town just past those hills." She turned abruptly, swayed, entertained the swirling black dots once again, and folded quite gracefully into his arms.

Arms full of bedraggled woman, Kane cursed the fates soundly and glanced off in the direction she had indicated. In that direction there was only one town close enough for her to have come from and that was Saquarra. And Saquarra was where he was headed. He would take her back there. No doubt someone was missing her.

He swung her up into the back of the wagon, trying to position her comfortably between the stacks of supplies that filled the back of the wagon. As he rearranged things, all he could think was that he had to get rid of her. This Samantha Cameron wasn't a responsibility he wanted on his hands. Working swiftly, he pulled a tin of grease from his storage box, smeared some quickly on her face, then pulled a lady's red and pink lace-trimmed bonnet from a hook, plopped it on her head, and nimbly secured the ribbons beneath her chin. Next he unrolled several lengths of fabric from one of the bolts and fashioned a sort of tent to shield her from the sunlight that filtered through the openings at the front and back ends of the wagon, fastening the ends of the material to the wagon's side posts on which he hung his wares. Finally, he poured a few drops of tepid water from a canteen over her lips and into her mouth, propping the nearly full container beside her before he collected his rifle and climbed back up on the wagon box.

Reins once again comfortably draped between his long, dexterous fingers, Kane clucked to the horse "Come on, Buck, we've got to take a lady home, and I want to be quick about it."

The horse responded by pricking up his ears, tossing his head, and stepping out lively.

They had been rolling a couple of hours when Kane drew the wagon to an easy halt and checked the woman's condition. She was not awake, but she seemed to be breathing easy. He dribbled some more water into her mouth, then resumed the journey.

The wagon was rumbling steadily along when Samantha half roused herself, bracing an elbow on a feedsack enough to see out the back. She fingered the bonnet tied loosely on her head and made a face as her explorations found the grease plastered on cheeks, chin, and nose. It wasn't a pleasant discovery, but what energy the night's trek had not drained, the sun had sucked from her. She was too weary to care. All she could register was that the wagon was moving. Wherever they were going was all right with her. She sank back down into the comparative comfort of the peddler's wares, her eyes drooping shut once more, lulled by the rhythm of the rumbling wheels.

By the time Samantha woke again, the sun had crested its zenith and was trekking off to the west. That was to say, the sun hung at their backs and the wagon was moving steadily east, a fact Samantha's exhausted mind finally grasped when Saquarra hove into view over the driver's shoulder through the front of the wagon. She frantically twisted around trying to get a better view, unable to believe her eyes.

Kane was aware of her wakening due to the noises coming to him from the back of the wagon. He turned in her direction, allowing the horse to pick his own path.

"Looks like you finally woke up. Missed most of the ride. We've almost got you home."

"It's not home."

"You said you came from Saquarra."

"*Came* from."

Kane was quiet a few moments while the wagon rumbled closer to the town.

"What were you doing out there?"

"Leaving Saquarra!"

Kane felt the statement like a mule kick. "Well, hell," was his only response. Plainly this was trouble.

"Couldn't you head somewhere else?" Samantha asked. "Saquarra is not a very friendly town. You won't be welcomed."

"Everybody welcomes a peddler."

"Not Saquarra."

"Well, hell," Kane repeated to himself.

Samantha sighed, then raised her voice above the banging of his peddler's wares, set into motion by an inconvenient rock beneath the wagon's wheel. "Hey," she yelled, "what's your name?"

"Zachariah Kane," he replied without the usual hesitation of most Western men. "Why? You want it to put on my tombstone?"

He did not know how close he was to the truth. There was no telling what Mississippi Pike would do if he saw her riding into town with this strange man, peddler or not. There was the possibility that in his high opinion of himself Pike had not yet even gotten around to seriously believing she would not come crawling back. She was going to have to brazen it out, crawl up there on that driver's box alongside the peddler, and look Mississippi Pike straight in the eye.

No she wasn't! Samantha, feeling suddenly dizzy, gave a slow moan, and slid back down amongst the cloth and sacks, eyes closed.

"Ma'am? Ma'am?" Kane looked over his shoulder to see Samantha curled again amongst his wares, unresponsive as the wagon rolled into Saquarra. He turned back and clucked to his horse.

"Come on, Buck. I think that sun was harder on her than we thought. We best find this little lady a doc."

CHAPTER
THREE

The sleepy little desert town was situated on a broad flat, tucked just west of a cluster of imposing cactus-covered hills. It had been baking quietly beneath the early afternoon sun when the wagon rattled in. Kane let the horse just keep walking at that familiar, dogged pace, and he utilized the time to size up the place. It was obvious to him that anyone approaching the dusty little town would be observed for miles. More, he had the uneasy feeling his approach had been closely watched. His senses prickled and sharpened, and he remembered his passenger had said he would not be welcome in Saquarra.

Sound carries far on the clear desert air. Sharp, annoying sound carries even farther. When the peddler's wagon rolled into Saquarra, the crash-banging sounds of Zachariah's wares, still jouncing from the wagon's rocky encounter, had preceded them. A crowd was being drawn into the street to greet his arrival.

Kane's golden eyes narrowed just a bit, aware of — but not watching too closely — the jocular folks spilling into the street to turn the arrival of a peddler into a carnival. There was a lot of laughter and a few sharp whistles. Kane was most interested in the few faces in the crowd that remained stiff, eyes locked on him and his wagon, evaluating him. They kept back of the more congenial townspeople.

A small pack of town dogs, large and small, attracted by turning wheels and loud noises bounced and yapped alongside the wagon until Kane's horse began to prance with nervousness.

"Hiya, pups! You get away now." Kane's gruff voice cut through the surrounding din. "That horse of mine is tuckered enough without you nippin' at his heels."

He sat easy on the box, eyes flicking over the curious folks clustering around the slowly moving wagon. With his practiced peddler's smile he drew in the reins, bringing the wagon to a stop. The racket quelled the instant the wagon rolled to a halt.

"Greetings to you, folks," he called out. "I'm an independent merchant, and I have lots of goods to share with you. But first, I found a young woman out in the desert. She says she came from here. She's in the back, and I think she needs a doctor."

It was about as long a speech as he cared to make, but it spread silence over the crowd and drew a young woman forward. With a puzzled expression on her face she peered into the back of the wagon.

"Why that's Samantha Cameron!" she cried, taking a step back and clutching at a shawl draped closely about her shoulders, as if fearing contact with something unspeakable.

Reins dangling loosely from his hands, Kane was suddenly aware of the passage of a hot wind between wooden buildings, the still nervous stamping of his horse, and the jingling of the bridle as the sorrel gelding tossed his head. He gave the wooden constructions an appraising glance. Timber, used for building, was unusual in a country where most shops and houses were made from mud.

The silence echoed. Then a ripple of conversation spread through those gathered, and a couple of people in the crowd simply turned and walked away.

"You folks got anything here that passes for a doc?"

Low, muttered, unintelligible responses came until a boy's youthful voice called out above the others. "We've got us a doc, but he's gone as usual. Today he's out at the Mitchell spread."

"Not that he'd touch *her!*" an indignant female voice snapped from the fringes of the crowd.

"Doc'd help anybody who needs it," the boy replied.

"Won't do me much good if he's not here, son," Kane responded. "Anybody else who can help this lady?"

"*Lady?* Hah!" The woman who earlier had been so eager to pass judgment stepped forward from the thinning crowd, pointed chin elevated, nose stiffly thrust in the air, small black eyes damning. "I say leave her in the street until Mississippi Pike sees fit to pick up his trash!"

The boy, a thin youth dressed in a boy's usual mismatched, dirt-begrimed, and ripped clothes, moved boldly up to the wagon, gaining himself a look into the back. "Yep," he affirmed to the few people remaining, "it's Miss Samantha." He cocked his head, appraising

26

Kane, then apparently judging him worthy he gave a rebellious grin. "You might try over to Mex-town. Might find a *curandera* there who'll nurse her if you pay."

Kane frowned, staring at the few remaining people lingering near the wagon. A couple of the hard cases had disappeared as well, but that somehow worried, more than reassured, him. He turned to check on Samantha. She was conscious again and slowly sitting up in the back of the wagon. A short, bandy-legged man with a thick crop of rusty hair and a possessive air appeared out of nowhere, reaching up to guide or drag her down — it was a little hard to determine which. What was not hard for Kane to ascertain was that the man's small, black eyes, set in an angular face, looked no different than those of the sidewinder he had teased from beneath Samantha's skirts. He sensed the attention of those remaining riveted on them.

Kane read trouble in the set of the man as he climbed down from the wagon. Somehow the self-styled cocky badman didn't seem Samantha's type. Still, she accepted his attentions with a wary stiffness. The handful of remaining spectators perked up and were somberly and tensely awaiting the outcome of this little drama.

Samantha spoke quickly in low, urgent tones, indistinct to everyone except the man gripping her arm. Her back was to him so Kane could not read the expression on her face, but the man was eyeing him with cold displeasure. It was the look of a hunting cat eyeing a mouse. Even though Samantha was addressing him, his malignant glare was fixed over the curve of her shoulder on Kane.

"She says you picked her up in the desert, didn't do nothin' but give her a ride back here. Might've saved her life. You reckon I owe you some kind of debt for that, stranger?"

"No. I was headed this way. Glad to give her a hand."

"Please, Mississippi, I told you. I went for a ride yesterday and got lost. Mister Kane helped. That's all."

Though her expression never changed, Samantha was curling up inside. She had learned never to allow Mississippi Pike even to glimpse her emotions. The damned peddler had brought her back to the very place she did not want to be. She ought to let things play out without interfering. Presently she would have quite enough trouble of her own.

"She's been gone all night." Pike's words sagged and drawled with meaning. "Now you come draggin' tail in here with her in your wagon just as pretty as you please. I don't like it. Pretty little teacher's my property. Mississippi Pike's property, and I'm thinkin' maybe I owe you somethin'."

This was when he was expected to grovel at Pike's feet, swear he had never touched the woman, and that he would be out of town before Pike got off the street with his property. Trouble was, Kane had never been much on considering women as property. And it was not in Kane to grovel. Every man drew a line for himself; here was where Kane's lay.

"The lady told you what happened." Kane shrugged the reply like it was the least important thing on his mind.

"Lady! Haw!"

Kane decided there and then that Samantha had shown good sense if Pike had been the reason she had left Saquarra. He knew Pike's breed well. Nothing less than a belligerent weasel, probably playing second fiddle to someone else's number one, so filled with his own self-importance that he was apt to have the disposition of a rabid wild hog. There was another trademark of the breed, and Kane, traveling from town to town, had seen his share close up. Almost all of them were inclined to be kill-crazy. The whole town knew it, too. They were waiting — some on the street and some behind cracked shutters.

Kane wore no sidearm. His rifle was still under the driver's box of the wagon. The muscles tightened along the back of his neck and across his shoulders. Then he leaned casually against the side of the wagon, nerves stretched taut, eyes calmly fixed on Pike and waiting. But not for long.

Pushing Samantha aside with a firm thrust, Pike planted himself squarely in front of the peddler with an air of superiority and command. Samantha stayed where she had been put, staring at Kane, her eyes eloquently apologizing.

"I don't like no man messin' around where I already staked my claim." Pike announced as he swaggered a step nearer the peddler. "From where I stand that means you owe me an apology."

"Mississippi . . . ," Samantha attempted. Why she was trying to help the peddler even she couldn't understand. She was unsteady on her feet, weaving like grass in a soft breeze, and Pike wouldn't listen to her anyway — he had no reason to. "He's just a peddler who gave me a ride back to town. Nothing happened."

Pike rounded on her, hand held aloft as if ready to strike. Samantha flinched and backed up a step in a reflexive move that caused Kane to lift an eyebrow in disquiet.

"Then why the hell you defendin' him thisaway?"

"She's not telling you anything but the truth," Kane interjected. "A blind man could see as much."

"You tryin' to make me out to seem the fool here?"

"No man can do that to another," Kane replied calmly.

"Mississippi . . . ," Samantha began again in a reasonable tone.

"Shut up!" Pike growled, not bothering to turn to face her, perhaps fearing to leave his back exposed. "I'll settle with you later."

Samantha withered, yet her pale eyes flashed a sharp warning in Kane's direction. She had not counted on the peddler putting himself in a position to be killed. That, though, seemed the direction in which the man was heading. Yet, there was nothing she could do for the fool peddler — and that was what he was. She wished he would just back down and pull out. She felt a tremor pass the length of her body. She knew she had stuck her neck out much too far already. Pike would remember her attempts to stick up for the peddler once he was through with Kane. Her miserable conscience could nag at her all it liked. She had to concentrate on deflecting Pike's wrath from herself.

Kane eyed the man, standing spraddle-legged before him, weighing how hard he should push. This was not at all the way he had figured on entering Saquarra. But he would not back down, for with Mississippi Pike that would include leaving town *pronto* like a whipped dog. *Damn it,* he thought, casting Samantha a side-long glance, *she could have warned him!* — then again, he should have guessed.

"Drummers," Pike was sneering. "Peddlers. Always full of big words and fancy speeches. Seems to me somebody ought to take the time to deal with 'em. Might even be a kindness . . . wiping out the whole stinking breed."

Kane concentrated on those beady eyes and the set of his adversary's body. He saw it coming almost before Mississippi had completed his thought. Pike stepped into it and threw a roundhouse punch at Kane's head.

Kane gripped a tin pan and swung it clear of the wagon tarp, its surface flashing brightly in the light of the westering sun just before it caught the full force of Pike's blow in its center. The pan clanked dully. Pike swore bitterly. Kane shifted sideways along the length of the wagon, backing up as Pike advanced, both wounded pride and fury etched into the lines of his narrow face.

"You ain't worth one of my bullets, peddler. I'm gonna take you apart with my own two hands!"

Kane dodged when Pike came at him again. He caught most of the blow on a rounded shoulder, then dropped to the dust, and rolled beneath the wagon. He was rolling through to the other side, coming up on hands and knees, when Pike skirted the back of the wagon and threw a vicious kick at Kane's head. He caught the boot in mid-swing, gave it a wrench, and Pike was down in the dust beside him, snarling grim epithets, attempting to throttle him when a gruff voice ripped through the air like a dull knife, punctuated by the sharp crack of a gunshot.

"That's about enough!" the voice commanded.

Face to face with Pike, Kane was aware of the anger blazing high in the other man's little pig eyes. In another moment a large, square figure loomed, then bent to drag them apart. Kane caught the brunt of it but chose not to protest when he saw the silver glint of the sheriff's badge on the burly man's chest. He settled for coming quickly to his feet.

"You lookin' to get yourself shot, Brown?" Pike asked as he climbed to his feet, grinding out the words like they were nuts with hard shells.

"You know what Crockett said about trouble here in town," the sheriff reminded Mississippi gruffly. "He wants it nice and peaceful. If he finds out you started something, he'll have your hide."

"Listen Brown," Mississippi said menacingly, "I know what Frank Crockett wants and don't want. That badge you're wearin' ain't worth spit, and you know it. So back off before you find out what real trouble is!"

32

The scattering of the town's people, riveted to their places only a few seconds before, was disappearing as quickly as prairie dogs diving for their burrows. The sheriff's arrival took all the excitement out of the encounter, and from this point on it could get raw and deadly.

The people of Saquarra were a peculiar breed, Kane decided. As far as he could see, there was nothing to stop Mississippi Pike from plugging the sheriff and doing the same to him. But then, he had not yet seen the second-floor window of the hotel across the street slide open and a solitary figure appear, leaning his hands on the wooden window sill and puffing slowly on an over-size cigar. Sheriff Clive Brown and Mississippi Pike, though, had an unrestricted view of the broad, sun-browned face with its thick, neatly trimmed mustache and its stony set. The man they watched uttered no sound, but his presence spoke volumes. Framed in the window, he watched, broad, beefy shoulders amply filling the frame, his casual look deceiving.

Their steady stares drew Kane's attention. He risked a look in an upward direction, catching a glimpse of a man in the window, turning his broad, white-shirted back on the street below and then disappearing from view.

Frank Crockett was not a man to be taken lightly under any circumstances. It was his silent appearance on the scene that had dispersed the citizens and not the sheriff's showy entrance. Kane was still looking intently at the now empty window when Pike turned on him again. This time, though, his anger was contained in his words, instead of his fists.

"Looks like you're gettin' off easy, peddler," he snarled, still nursing his stinging hand which had connected with the tin pan. "Reckon the law dog here is right this time." His words were filled with contempt for both the man and the badge. "But you better stay out of my way. In fact, it might be wise for you to just clear on out of here *pronto.*"

Mississippi turned on his heel abruptly. He grabbed Samantha roughly by one arm and dragged her across the street and into the block-long saloon. Kane saw Samantha flinch again, this time because of Pike's firm grip on the sun-scorched skin of her arm. Her dusty gingham skirts disappeared into the shadows before Kane looked away.

It seemed obvious the sheriff was not worth much in Saquarra, but it was equally discernible that he had learned to take advantage of whatever edge he had with the canny calculation of an Apache. He might not have the real authority that went with the badge he wore, but he had learned the art of survival in a town like Saquarra. He gave Kane a guarded look.

"He'll be laying for you, just waiting for an excuse to kill you. Mississippi likes killing." The sheriff shrugged. "Might be for the best if you were to take his advice and push on."

After his run-in with Pike, Kane knew that time spent in Saquarra from now on was going to be parlous in the extreme. He felt guilty about bringing Samantha back. Up until his encounter with Pike, he'd just wanted to be shut of her, to pass on the responsibility of caring for her. Now, in fact, he felt more keenly responsible for her well-being than he had on the trail. Maybe he owed her something, after all. He felt he better stick around a while. But first he had to get a better feel for the lay of the land.

"I have business here."

Sheriff Brown frowned. "Can't be that important."

"Matter of opinion, Sheriff."

"Got a handle you go by?"

"Kane, Zachariah Kane."

"Well, Zachariah Kane, why don't you get your wagon and come on over to the jail. I'll buy you a drink, and we can have a talk. Maybe I can change your mind."

"You can't, Sheriff, but I could sure use that drink." Kane moved to his horse, laying a hand on his bridle to lead him across the street.

They started walking, the dust rising from beneath their boots and curling up on either side of the wagon.

"Well then, that's a mighty fine name you spouted," the sheriff resumed. "It'll look real good on the marker we'll carve for you. You can just put it down on a piece of paper . . . you know, proper, for me."

That was the second time in one day his name had been linked with a marker. Kane grinned to himself and ambled along with the sheriff toward the jail.

CHAPTER
FOUR

The room was enveloped in the gathering shadows of mid-afternoon, except for one corner where a lamp hung from the ceiling, burning softly with a low flame, casting off fine tendrils of dark smoke and a yellow pool of light. Sitting beneath it behind a large oak desk, Frank Crockett raised squared fingers to twirl slowly a dark, fat cigar between his lips while he focused his attention on the darker shadings at the opposite end of the room, nearer the window overlooking the street below. Mississippi Pike lounged there, eyes fixed on the scene below him. His back was toward Crockett, and he appeared unconcerned with his boss's commanding presence. His pose was just that. His backbone rigid, he stared out on the street below from the exact vantage point Crockett himself had used earlier.

Crockett, his amber eyes glowing like a stalking cat's, held Pike in his concentrated gaze with the air of a judge about to pronounce sentence. But he said nothing. He waited instead, his broad face expressionless, immobile as stone, his eyes intense, heated, beneath thick sun-bleached eyebrows.

Mississippi Pike had come quickly enough at Crockett's summons, as most anyone with any sense in

Saquarra would have done. Crockett, with some satisfaction, had noted that fact. But Pike, save a grunted greeting, had said nothing since his arrival. Pike did not have the brains of a prairie chicken as far as Crockett could see, but he could be very dangerous. Although Crockett acknowledged that in the man, he did not fear him. Even at such times as this he tolerated his *segundo*'s posturing.

Frank Crockett was head man in Saquarra. Mississippi was one of his original bunch. It was Frank who had devised the setup in Saquarra, and he made it plain to any new arrivals how things stood. His authority had only been tested a couple of times. Each time he acted with all the swiftness and venom of a striking snake, putting the matter quickly to rest.

Finally, Pike turned deliberately toward his boss, his beady little eyes shining like black opals alight with internal fire. "She's my woman, bought and paid for," he spat without preamble, his voice cold. "I want that peddler dead."

Crockett waited a moment before removing the cigar from between his lips. He watched the smoke curling slowly toward the light overhead as quiet settled again in a thick pall between them. "You know what we've got here in Saquarra," he said at last, his voice a low rumble against the viscous silence of the big room. "We don't need any outside attention drawn to us. Besides, the locals wouldn't appreciate your starting to gun down peddlers that come through just because you don't like peddlers. What do you think would happen?"

With his right hand Crockett eased the top drawer of his desk open. Pike shrugged and his eyes slid away from Crockett's like water skittering across oil.

"It's a good thing I kept Sheriff Brown on," Crockett continued in the same tone. "He sure as hell doesn't want us here, but the townsfolk do, and he doesn't want his town blown apart. He knows where to draw the line and how to keep a town quiet. He's cut you off a couple of times now, Mississippi. The town's good folks are beginning to worry about you."

The smoke from his cigar curled up on a draft. Crockett looked from Pike to the Colt double-action revolver nestled in the desk's top drawer, then back to Pike. He left the drawer open, his hand hanging over its edge, fingers within reach of the gun.

"Let 'em worry," Mississippi snorted. "Maybe they'll develop some backbone."

"That," Crockett growled, "is exactly what we don't want them to do." His fingers gripped the end of the cigar with a strength that was flattening it out. In a tone of a flat command he said a little more quietly: "Leave the peddler alone." His fingers twitched near the butt of the Colt.

Pike bridled under the order. He resented it when Crockett took it upon himself to lay down an edict.

"I reckon I hear you, but this ain't got nothin' to do with the town. This is personal."

"As long as we have this setup, nothing is personal. You take your orders from me."

"You ain't got no right to question me."

The smoke from Crockett's cigar made lazy swirls in the golden lamplight, and the big man squinted into the haze, hand now curled firmly around the butt of the Colt. Some day, perhaps soon, he was going to have to shoot Mississippi — and make damned sure he was dead. "I'm not questioning you. I'm giving an order."

Pike's hand rested on his hip very near his own gun. He had never been able to read subtleties in men. There had never been much need. Blundering through life, he took what he wanted and usually got what he was after. Looking down the bore of his six-shooter had nearly always been persuasion enough for those who stood in his way. He'd been a shootist for a few years and rode with a couple of gangs, finally teaming up with Crockett. They had seemed to have the same basic approach to life, though Crockett had more of an eye toward when to let things be, when not to press an advantage. To Pike's way of thinking there was never such an instance.

Now he had to answer to Frank Crockett. At times like these even that was too much. A few months back he had caught hell from Crockett after he had gunned down a gambler in the saloon. Mississippi swore the man was cheating at cards, though he could find nothing in the dead man's hand or the deck to indicate how he had been accomplishing it. Still, gamblers who traveled around from town to town were bound to be cheating more often than not. Besides, Crockett had been far more angry with a few of the other boys who had had a run-in with a couple of the townspeople in the same saloon only a few nights before. That incident had resulted in one of the townsmen being badly beaten, another dead. Crockett had managed to quiet the matter down, but it had left the townsfolk jittery and questioning.

"Reckon I knew what I was getting into when I hooked up with you and the bunch," Pike finally responded. "Reckon bein' your number two man I can do you a favor now and again, but you better keep your tongue behind your teeth when you think to start shoutin' orders."

Crockett's hand relaxed around the butt of the Colt. The smile he gave Mississippi was cool and empty. "I just want to hear you're going to leave the peddler alone," he repeated slowly. "Either believe the woman or get rid of her, but don't kill because of her." He paused. "She ran out on you last night, didn't she?"

"Aw, she wasn't gonna get far," Mississippi countered uneasily. "I knew she was gonna come crawlin' back. She's a woman. She just took a notion, that's all."

"Then I don't have to worry about you shooting the peddler on sight?"

Pike narrowed his eyes and stood in front of Crockett's desk, his own hand easing down beside the low-slung holster on his right hip, away from the gun butt, fingers curling in a relaxed attitude. "I'll let him keep breathin' a while longer if he keeps away from Samantha. He looks cross-eyed in her direction . . . we'll have us another go-'round."

Nodding silently in reply, Crockett infuriated the cocky shootist with his calm, patronizing acceptance of his statement without further comment. He merely withdrew his hand from his desk drawer, easing it closed, and leaned back in his chair until the springs creaked.

"Mississippi," he added as Pike turned to leave, "don't get any ideas about pushing the sheriff into a gun fight either."

Pike grunted something unintelligible in reply as he stepped toward the door, pausing, his hand on the knob. Because he had risen to the accepted position of Crockett's right hand man, he had made a few concessions, but Frank Crockett could die as easily as any other man. Pike was beginning to think of the probabilities of sliding into Crockett's position without so much as a protest from the rest of the men.

"I ain't givin' no promises where that sheriff is concerned. He's baitin' me."

Crockett regarded Mississippi appraisingly over the glowing tip of his cigar. "Then stay away from him."

Pike's hand hovered by the knob a moment longer. There were times when Crockett could be unnerving. It was as if the man could read minds. He had been chewing on the idea of taking the sheriff in a fair gun fight. He figured Crockett could not fault him for gunning the man in self-defense. Gunning down Sheriff Brown now, after Crockett's warning, would be crossing his direct order, a dangerous thing to do as long as Crockett had the backing he held. Pike swore under his breath, turned the knob, and started down the hall. Taking the stairs two at a time, he burst through the lobby and into the street. Turning in the direction of the saloon, he moved even faster. He needed a drink and some time to think things out.

Frank Crockett rose from his chair beneath the lamp and, still puffing thoughtfully on his cigar, moved to the window as Mississippi stepped out onto the street, headed for the saloon. Samantha Cameron would soon have a visitor. Though Pike wore a mask of calm, he was furious with the woman, and Crockett wondered if she would be able to handle Pike in his present state. Especially after his own little talk with Mississippi which had fanned the fires of his anger even higher. He hoped she could.

The little teacher was a beautiful woman compared to when she'd been hauled into town — bruised, battered, and smelling to high heaven. Somehow Pike had seen the possibilities beneath the dirt and stench and had gone after her like a wolf scenting a sage hen. Over time Pike's obsession with the woman had grown all out of proportion. Though women appealed to Crockett, and Samantha was now a shining jewel in this town of dull pebbles, he would not kill over a woman. At the time Pike had bought her from the marauding Mexicans, Crockett had just sat back, watched with interest, and waited. And, based on what he had seen these last months, Crockett believed Samantha Cameron could easily be convinced to take a hand against Pike.

He remained standing at the darkened window, staring at the lively street below. It was busy, not only with the town's citizens but with the men the town in its uniqueness had brought in — outlaws, bandits, men

42

with known faces and names, men on their way to becoming known. Saquarra had become a sanctuary for them, a place where they could stop running and rest, at least for a while, without looking over their shoulders. Crockett and his men represented the only permanent residents who functioned outside the law.

Saquarra had been a small, isolated town near the border with a problem much too large for it to cope with alone, and no help had been forthcoming. Its position had placed it just right to be a prime target for raids by Mexican *bandidos,* roaming outlaws needing a stake, and the Apaches whose entire life style revolved around raiding and counting coup on their enemies. Saquarra had been hit by them all and was on the brink of disaster. Then Frank Crockett had stumbled onto the little town while headed north out of Mexico.

He tossed the remaining stub of his cigar aside, remembering their fateful arrival in the former mining town. He had realized a golden opportunity existed in Saquarra and, posing as a former lawman and ex-vigilante, had made a proposition to the beleaguered citizens. He had a group of men, "assistants" he had called them, whom he could call in to assure safety for the citizens. He offered protection to the town for a nominal monthly fee as long as he and his "assistants" were needed.

The majority of the citizenry of Saquarra were enthused with the idea, welcoming with open arms relief in any form in preference to the state of siege under which they had been living. Others, including Sheriff Clive Brown, had been reluctant and had stood their ground against Crockett and his men. The desire of the majority had prevailed.

Crockett had called in his men, and they had gone to work immediately, protecting the town from the human predators it feared. Two of Crockett's ten original men were lost during the early skirmishes that had ensued. Yet in the end he and his men had not merely beaten the attacks off, they had, in many instances, run the aggressors to the ground and settled with them permanently. Saquarra acquired a reputation as a place with more crust than an armadillo. Then peace had settled over the desert town like a calm breeze.

It wasn't long before another change came along to Saquarra. Strangers had drifted into town in increasing numbers and had been neatly escorted out. Then Crockett had left town briefly. He had returned to find the saloon catering to the thirst of several Mexican bandits who had crossed the border on the run from the *Rurales*. Those left in charge during his absence had maintained order by riding tight herd on the newcomers. The bandits had arranged to meet with Crockett. They had offered recompense for a temporary haven. And they had promised to behave.

Staring out the window to the lighted street below, Crockett smiled. After that he had set a price on sanctuary, and Saquarra had taken on a new life. Lawless men from two countries willing to pay the price then had drifted in and out of the small, isolated town. His income had more than doubled. Crockett had lost another man to an old grudge fight, but it had been a fair fight, and he had let it go.

Crockett had kept on good terms with Sheriff Brown but had maintained his distance. Brown handled the small disturbances at the saloon and an occasional fight elsewhere. Within the circle of his authority Crockett had become the undisputed town boss. Money had flowed into the suddenly prospering town, and life had become much easier. The cemetery was growing, but, except for the man killed in the saloon brawl, the names on the tombstones belonged to strangers instead of family and friends as had formerly been the case when Saquarra had been raided on a regular basis.

Only a handful of the town's citizens realized Saquarra no longer belonged to them, and they were in no position to attempt to do anything about it. They would have to fight not only the outlaws, but most of the good citizens of Saquarra who found the new order preferable to the old. Men who had chosen their path rarely had either the inclination or the guts to admit they had been wrong. Neither would they be apt to make changes a second time so soon.

The saloon lights from the far side of the street were bright and beckoning. Crockett shrugged into his coat and started for the door. He was sure of his town, of his power over it. Pike was his only immediate problem, and he would be dealt with in time. It was of little significance. The most important thing on Crockett's mind now was a long tall beer.

CHAPTER
FIVE

With trepidation Samantha eased down into her hip-bath, filled with tepid water and infused with oatmeal meant to take the sting and heat out of her sunburn. What she had seen in the mirror upon her return to her room had been distressing. The pale, evenly-toned skin of her face which had been her strongest source of pride for many years was seared a brilliant red. Next, as she slowly undressed, she discovered that her upper body, where the fabric had been only a thin covering, was also burned but to a lesser degree. Where her skin had been fully exposed — her face, throat, and arms — the sun's damage was severe. She gained some comfort from the fact that she had not been touched by the sun from the waist down. As she lowered her body into the tub, she studied the contrast between her arms and her long, pale legs. Once settled, she scooped the creamy waters over her upper torso. Her body shivered as the heat radiated out of it. The shivering was intensified by the thought of Mississippi Pike.

She had been relieved when Pike had left her alone in her room. But she could not escape the dread she felt over the fact that he would inevitably return and confront her about her attempt to leave him — and about the peddler. Samantha tried not to think about Pike since he would return soon enough. There had been whispers that he had been summoned to Crockett's office. A meeting with Crockett would no doubt add to his fury. She winced as she scooped a double-handful of the soothing water over her face once, then again. The sting abated momentarily as she eased down into the water, allowing her hands and arms total submersion.

Over the last thirty-six hours fate had conspired against her in her efforts to rid herself of Mississippi Pike and Saquarra, once and for all. Instead of being miles from the town now, she was right back where she had started. She hated everything about this town in which she was an outcast. The citizens were probably as disappointed in her return as was she. From the minute of her initial arrival in Saquarra, the women had had nothing to do with her. That wasn't surprising. The whispers began almost at once — "Pike's whore." The men weren't much better. They occasionally ventured a furtive, lustful glance in her direction, if they thought he wasn't around or looking, but basically they feared Pike's jealous and irrational nature.

Samantha knew not a single soul she could call friend in Saquarra. Its newest inhabitant, the peddler, seemed reluctant to become too involved. She had sensed his reluctance even out on the desert. There was little chance that he would provide any assistance now that she was actually back in Saquarra and under Pike's watchful eye.

She glanced toward the window. The afternoon shadows were gathering into evening, the sky turning a pale peach, glowing with the promise of much richer colors to come. Life held no promise for her. It hadn't for some time now. She thought of the filthy Mexican bandits who had started it all by hauling her, unwillingly, to this twisted dusty little town. If she had just been on another stagecoach . . . ?

The silence of the desert was interrupted by the sound of pounding hoofbeats. The stagecoach began to slow down. Samantha raised the cover over the coach window, that kept out the dust somewhat, and ventured a glance outside. She could see five men, Mexicans, galloping toward the stagecoach. She quickly let the cover drop, her head pounding.

The stage came to a lurching halt, and one of the men shouted something in Spanish at the driver and the guard. Then two shots rang out. The doctor inside the coach with Samantha looked across at her with sympathy in his eyes. Then his attention returned to focus on his lap where he fidgeted with his pocket watch. There was more shouting outside the stage. Time seemed to stand still. Then, more shots.

Finally the door was wrenched open. Orders were shouted at Doctor Henry Wilder which Samantha could not understand. Whether the doctor understood or not, he alighted from the stage, and Samantha's heart sank. One of the Mexicans stuck his head inside the stage. He leered at Samantha and reached out to touch her. Samantha slid as far out of his reach as she was able, her body overcome with a disgusted shuddering. The man laughed, the stench of his sour breath filling the interior of the stage, and then closed the door. Within several moments there was the sound of another gunshot. Samantha waited. It sounded as if someone were climbing up into the driver's box, and then the stage was moving again, although its path was now a series of dizzying circles. Laughter from the murderers filled the air, as the remainder of the men, now remounted, rode near the stage, taunting Samantha.

The Mexicans kept up their torturous antics for hours. The stage would head first in one direction and then another, sometimes just making those dizzying circles. Inside Samantha sat paralyzed, gripping the edge of the seat with whitened knuckles. Her only desire was to spring out of the door and fling herself onto the desert floor, ending this torment. But she couldn't bring herself to do it and continued to cling. As day turned into night, she could contain herself no longer, and she began to scream.

The stage finally stopped. Samantha was yanked out and thrown on the ground. Still she screamed. The screaming only stopped when she was knocked unconscious by a well-placed clout on the side of her head with a gun barrel. When she came to, a small camp fire was crackling, and the smell of beans permeated the air around the camp site. When she saw the five sets of eyes staring at her, she began to scream again. One of the five men slowly drew himself up to a standing position and made his way toward her, a gun in one hand and a bottle of tequila in the other. He snapped her up to a sitting position by her arm and placed the muzzle of the gun against her forehead. The steel felt icy cold against her skin. The man, whom the others coaxed on, they addressed as Manuel.

Glancing back at his friends with a grin on his face, Manuel thrust the mouth of the bottle to Samantha's lips which brought the screams to a stop as it chipped her front teeth. The tip of the gun was pushed more firmly against her forehead, forcing her to tip back her head, allowing a small amount of the liquid to flow into her mouth. Samantha began to choke, and she pushed the gun aside. Her eyes began to water, and she gagged. Manuel slid down to a crouch next to her and forced the bottle to her lips again, the gun merely aimed at her, no longer touching her skin. She shook her head. The gun was cocked. She took a small swallow of the pale amber liquid. One of the four men across from the fire made a smacking noise which made all of them laugh. Manuel raised the bottle to Samantha's lips again and again . . .

It was a combination of the bright morning sun and the intense pounding behind her eyes that awakened Samantha. She tried to lift her head but was overwhelmed by dizziness, and she began to retch. The feeling passed after several minutes, and she felt better. As she lay her head back, she caught movement out of the corner of her eye. There were men riffling through the baggage on the stage. The events of yesterday and the night before slowly fell into place in Samantha's liquor-fogged brain.

"Oh, my God," she whispered in a sickened moan as she recalled the attack on the stagecoach, the killings, and later the burn of the liquid running down her throat, the giddy, warm feeling that eventually followed, and finally the slobbery kisses and insistent gropings of the men . . . She vomited on herself.

Over the following six days Samantha was kept in varying states of drunkenness as they traveled in a southerly direction. This circumstance combined with a lack of food and the intense heat served to take all the fight out of her. The days were spent passively tied in the stage; her nights were pure hell. Samantha thought she would go mad. Perhaps she already had.

One morning the wagon was burned. Two of the men rode away that night and returned with a stranger, an Anglo, many hours later. His rusty-colored hair looked soft and clean to Samantha, not unkempt and dirty like the others, standing around her. As the fair-skinned man stared at her, she tried to appear steady, even though the effects of the tequila made the sand beneath her feet shift up and down. A feeling of humiliation washed over her as she realized she must look a sight — her hair hadn't been combed in a week, and her dress, in addition to being torn, smelled sour from all the times she had been sick on it. The stranger then walked a small distance away with two of the men. They talked, and then he was gone. He returned some time later with a second horse, and Samantha was at last rescued.

The stranger — Mississippi Pike he called himself — took her to Saquarra where he lived. He made arrangements for her to stay in a room above the block-long saloon in the center of town, telling her the hotel was full up and failing to mention the boarding house at all. A bath was prepared, and her clothes were taken away to be destroyed. In their place she was given silk undergarments and a soft dressing gown. This man, Pike, had food sent up to her, and she was beginning to feel somewhat human again. It wasn't until later that evening, when she began to feel strange after drinking some coffee he had brought for her, that she began to doubt whether she indeed had been rescued.

Samantha shivered in the tub. To think that she had actually felt a surge of gratitude when she had first encountered Mississippi Pike! She really had been very naive. That hadn't lasted long. It hadn't taken her long at all to realize that Pike was slipping something, maybe laudanum, into her drinks to keep her in a weakened condition. Beyond the undergarments and the dressing gown she had been given no clothes and was held virtually a prisoner in the room. He had made no advances upon her until the second week. He became abusive when she tried to resist him. When she finally submitted, he was at least gentler and cleaner than had been the Mexicans.

For three weeks she stayed in the room above the saloon, too drugged to walk or see straight. Over that time word about her arrival had spread. Because she stayed in the room all the time and was never seen by anyone but Pike, it wasn't long before the people of Saquarra began to talk in whispers about "Pike's whore." Slowly the amounts of the drug she had been given were decreased. Upon occasion she was given a dress to wear. Her hair would be fixed by one of the prostitutes from the saloon, and then Pike would take her downstairs where he would parade around the room with her on his arm. Pike's show would never last long, and she would be taken back to her room where the dress would be swept away by another of the saloon girls, and Samantha would be left alone with her feeling of shame. Her reputation was established in the community without her ever having said a word in her own defense. For Pike she felt only hate, but she was grateful that in deference to his temper Crockett's other men and the outlaws left her alone. The problem was *everyone* left her alone out of fear of Pike once she was allowed to wander the streets of Saquarra.

The tub water was getting cooler, sending uncontrollable shivers through her. Samantha stood and stepped out of the tub, carefully blotting the droplets of water from her pink and red flesh and just as carefully easing into a cotton robe, belting it loosely at her waist.

Barely had she finished when the door to her room banged open. Mississippi stood framed in the doorway, pleased, it seemed, that he did not find it necessary to knock. Then he stepped inside, slamming the door behind him. Samantha stood frozen, gripping the top of her robe more closely about her tender throat. His eyes were as hard as granite, but his words were infinitely soft, nearly inaudible.

"Well, aren't you prim as a preacher's wife at a prayer meetin'. I mean, here you are coverin' yourself up in front of me. I bet you offered that peddler plenty."

"He gave me a ride back to town. That's all."

"I'll just bet he did. We're gonna have to have a talk, you an' me, about just why he had to give you that ride. Why you were out there to begin with." He stepped closer, reaching out to cup her chin in his hand. "You know a fickle woman and a good-shootin' man are apt to hurt someone. And I suspect it's that peddler you dragged back here with you."

"He's nothing to me."

Crockett's *segundo* released her chin and stalked stiffly around her. "Uhn-huh. Bet you think you were havin' yourself a real party, slippin' out on me."

"I wasn't having anything. I just wanted to go . . . to go where I was supposed to go in the first place. Before coming here. To be away from here."

"Hell! You expect me to believe that? You were runnin' out on me to find another man. That's about as bad as it can get. Runnin' out on me for nothin'. Why, that's even worse! You forget, I *own* you! I paid hard cash for you, and I ain't done with you yet."

The blow came quickly, a stinging slap to the face which sent a sudden surge of pain ripping through her and left a starkly white palm print against Samantha's flaming cheek. She gasped, but said nothing.

"That's good. I want you to keep your yap shut." He continued to strut around her. "Maybe this was a good thing to have happen. Maybe you got it out of your system. Maybe, if we're both lucky, you learned something from this. That Saquarra is my town. Mine and Crockett's. Anybody comin' in has to have our okay. The same with anybody goin' out. And there ain't nobody gonna help you, here or anywhere you'd be able to get to." He eyed her closely. "Am I gettin' through to you?"

He grabbed her arm for emphasis, shoving the loose robe sleeve up past her elbow which allowed direct contact, so that the pink coloring flared white beneath the pressure of his fingers.

"I *own* you! If I can't have you, nobody will. I'm your keeper. I own you. I want to hear you say it."

She could only manage a nod.

"Good. You're lucky I'm in a forgivin' mood." He let her arm go and stepped toward the door. "You want to teach so bad, you be nice to me an' maybe I'll let you teach some of them snot-nosed Mex kids on the other side of town." He opened the door. "I'll be back later."

Samantha shuddered as the door closed. She wanted to scream. She wanted to tell him what she really thought of him and of Crockett and the whole bunch in Saquarra, including the Mexicans! Instead, salty tears trailed down her face, stinging her raw cheeks, and she swore to herself she would find some way to escape.

The afternoon was waning as Kane made his way along the streets of Saquarra, continuing his exploration of the town and its people. The evening's coolness would keep them out for a while, before the night wore on and Saquarra's more rowdy element drove the locals inside to sanctuary, and the morning light once more washed the streets clean.

Earlier the sheriff had tried to talk him out of staying in Saquarra, but then, again, most sheriffs weren't too partial to strangers of any kind. Kane was a little surprised at himself. Ordinarily he wouldn't have argued the point. He would have left town soon enough. With everybody telling him to leave, it put in him the notion to stay for a while. And then there was the Cameron woman. He'd been so blamed blind that he brought her back to the very town she had been fleeing.

"Something on your mind, son?"

Kane, leaning against a post, started at the sheriff's voice so close beside him.

"Just thinkin' what a nice town this is."

"Wasn't ever that great. Now it's a snake pit."

"I think it has potential. You just got to rid it of the snakes. You know, I've been walkin' around some. Meeting some of the folks. Listened to their stories. Why, Saquarra might even be the town I've been lookin' for. Might be the place to light and settle."

The sheriff rubbed his chin, his whiskers giving off a sand-papery whisper. "Got all that out of an evening stroll, did you?"

Kane shifted uncomfortably inside his dandified peddler's clothes, pinching open the gritty and battered celluloid collar, rubbing his neck. He grinned at the sheriff. "That and plenty more. The good folks feel quite a bit like me. Seems like most of 'em would like to shed the clothes they're wearing now and come out brand new. These peddler's clothes have been pinchin' me for a time now, too. Could be, we're all ready for a change."

Sheriff Brown swept off his hat, scratched his pate, and resettled the hat at a rakish angle. "Did you look around? You know what you really saw?"

"A peaceful town with its share of troubles, like any other town."

"Well, we have something a little different here. You have to remember, it wasn't too long ago walking the streets of Saquarra was about as dangerous as walking through quicksand over hell. Crockett and his boys changed all that, and folks were grateful."

56

"Were?"

"Well, some of 'em still are. That's why Crockett knows everything that goes on in this town. By that I mean *everything*."

"I've pretty much seen the elephant. I've been moving around too long now. I'm getting weary of the long, empty times between settlements, Sheriff. You see, after the war I thought I couldn't go far enough or long enough away from people. It was hell. Home was hell. Maybe that's why I like this place. I like the folks here. In time this could be some place . . . well, hell, I'm ramblin' on now, ain't I?"

A new light was kindled in the sheriff's eyes as he regarded Kane. Respect or wariness, it was hard to tell which. After a few more moments he gave a sage nod.

"You best watch your back," Sheriff Brown observed matter-of-factly, laying his hand on top of the gun butt protruding from his holster.

"I'll take that advice."

"I ain't just talking about Crockett and his men, either."

"I wasn't thinking of them only."

"Right smart of you."

Together they stood a few moments in companionable silence, staring out over the street, as the evening shadows lengthened and darkened, and lamps were lit in the establishments catering to the town's night life.

"Time to make my rounds," Brown said, abruptly stepping into the street. "Care to walk with me, son?"

57

"Be pleased to, Sheriff," Kane said, stepping out to join him. "Best way to see a town is walking rounds with the local sheriff."

Clive Brown snorted. "You can butter me up later over a drink in the saloon."

They walked a few yards, the sheriff tipping his hat to the wife of the hotel's proprietor and exchanging pleasant greetings with the livery owner before he spoke again to Kane.

"You talked to Zeb Kraus, owner of the general store, yet?"

Matching the sheriff's leisurely pace, following the course his eyes took, up and down the street, probing into the narrow alleys between buildings, the peddler grinned. "Saw him first."

Clive raised an eyebrow. "You told him what you plan, and he ain't run you out of town yet?"

"Thinks it's a pretty good idea."

"G'wan!"

"I'm going to talk to him later about the possibility of buying him out. He claims he's a damn' good blacksmith and said Ben, over at the livery, has been pestering him to turn his hand to it again."

They walked on together, edging the street until the sheriff pointed toward the end of town where they were headed. "Mex-town over thataway. Good folks mostly. Maria Sanchez does laundry if you're of a mind to hire it out. Good family people."

He added that last remark when several children scattered across the street at a run, a couple of scraggly dogs bounding at their heels. A small boy separated himself from the pack, running up between Kane and the sheriff.

"Sheriff Clive! My *mamacita* wishes to know when the trading man will come with his wagon!"

The sheriff just shrugged. "I don't know, Alejandro."

"I'll be over tomorrow," Kane assured the child.

The boy ran off to deliver the news. Clive Brown directed their footsteps back toward the other end of town to complete his circuit.

CHAPTER
SIX

Zachariah Kane leaned his elbows on the dark, gleamingly polished bar — obviously the pride and joy of the owner of the place. He glanced into the mirror across from the bar as he sipped his tepid beer. He had modified his peddler's garb — allowing the baggy pants which were comfortable enough to sag over his boot-tops, but abandoning the shirt that was too tight as well as the celluloid collar in favor of an open-collared drover's shirt pulled from his own stock. He surprised himself at how much he liked the people in this town and at his own interest in their predicament. Besides, his horse needed a good rest, and he could use one as well. Folks here were eager to buy from him, and he was in no hurry to leave. Human nature held a certain fascination for him when he roused himself from the solitude of travel and took time to observe.

Beside him the town barber, a short solidly built man with thinning hair and quick brown eyes, met his gaze in the mirror as Samantha's reflection glided into view. She was clad in a demure and elegant gown of burgundy taffeta with a high-laced neck and wore a tight little smile upon her lips and a rather distracted look in her eyes. Kane thought he spotted a stiffness in her movements, as if the practiced glide was not quite as smooth as it normally was. He frowned. Sunburn — or something else?

"Quite a looker, ain't she," Saquarra's barber observed between sips of beer. "I mighta been interested myself, but now . . ." He shrugged. "She ain't nothing more'n a whore since she took up with that Pike fella."

Kane raised a heavy brown eyebrow and scratched his jaw through his beard. "Heard she didn't have much of a choice."

The barber smirked. "Don't a woman always have a choice?"

We like to think so, Kane thought as he lifted his beer glass to his lips again and drained it to the bottom. Only the foam was left behind to fleck his mustache.

Three days had passed since he had made his noisy entrance into town. Business had been brisk, his popularity rising on both sides of the deadline of demarcation which separated Mex-town from the rest of Saquarra. A peddler was generally not a very highly respected man, but he was accepted nearly everywhere in Saquarra without question. And word had already spread that he was lingering longer than an ordinary peddler was wont to do. There was a rumor spreading that he might be setting up a more permanent business in time. It was a rumor spawned by his own actions, particularly his talk with Zeb Kraus, owner of the general store.

That revelation had appeared to arouse the curiosity of everyone in town, everyone, that is, except for Samantha Cameron. Since their arrival in Saquarra and his confrontation with Pike, Kane had caught only occasional glimpses of her in and out of the saloon on Pike's arm. It was obvious she was taking pains to walk a wide path around him. He wasn't sure if she was protecting his hide or hers. Maybe it was both. It didn't really matter. Plenty of other things had diverted his attention over the past few days in Saquarra. Yet, he kept coming back to the fact that, if it wasn't for Samantha, he might have moved on by now. Once he'd learned how she had come to be in Saquarra, it wasn't in him to abandon her despite a desire to do so. It churned in his gut that he had brought her back.

The town wasn't completely a lost cause. Changes would inevitably come. A growing number of folks in Saquarra knew that Crockett was no better than the outcasts he harbored, and they were none too pleased about having to continue to pay him. Saquarra plainly needed a good teacher. By her own admission Samantha had provided that service before arriving in Saquarra. Change was the only constant Kane was aware of in life, and Saquarra was due for some.

He had spent much of his time in the saloon and general store, two prime sources for information, and the two places in town everyone was sure to pass through at one time or another. On the surface Saquarra had the look of any other sleepy little desert town. Not much seemed to be going on, its main excitement of late being his own clattering arrival. Yet, there was change afoot in Saquarra. It was just a matter of time. Beneath the calm surface of the town there was brewing a violent storm, but one that, if left uncontrolled, could be only destructive. The way Kane perceived it, the gathering anger of the good citizens over the murder of one of their own by one of Crockett's men might prove to be the outlaws' undoing. Given some direction, some suggestions, the folks of Saquarra might liberate themselves, and lives would be spared, though no matter how the wheel turned, people were likely to end up dead.

Kane set his beer glass down with a solid thump. Straightening from the bar, he pitched his voice to be heard well beyond the barber beside him. "Reckon I'll go check my horse and outfit before I turn in."

"No need to worry, peddler," the barber grunted into his glass. "It's a nice, safe town we've got here." He cast Kane a smile that was both knowing and chilling. His words were edged with sarcasm.

The barber was not a man Kane cared to get to know better. "Never hurts to keep an eye on things," he said, ending the exchange. He stepped away from the bar and headed out the batwings into the cool desert night.

Outlaws and bandits filled Saquarra's streets. They wandered about, patronizing businesses as if they weren't temporary but belonged. Things appeared to be peaceful. Kane wondered how badly the merchants and business owners would regret the loss of revenue that would inevitably occur with the dethroning of Crockett. Kane understood the plight that had driven the citizens to swing open the gates for every thief, murderer, and the worst manner of low-life that the country had to offer. But what they had not realized at the time was that one type of scum does not keep another at bay; it just breeds more. Kane had seen it happen before, and he remembered. He had been only sixteen when the Civil War had sucked him into its bloody maw, nineteen when he finally returned home. His town was overrun by scum. Looted, it was just a skeleton of what it had been. Nothing was the same. He had buried his mother and his younger brother and sister. It always made him sick to think about it, to remember.

At nineteen he had had only one response to the horror he saw and that was to get as far away as possible. He'd worked his way west, trading here and there along the way to buy necessities. Eventually he bought a wagon and started selling those same necessities along with a few luxuries to others. The years had passed, yet the horror of the war remained, etched in his mind just as vividly as on the day he had left what remained of his home town. For some reason Saquarra had brought back strongly those images. Perhaps it was the look of defeat he saw on so many faces in Saquarra — especially on Samantha's, whose features bore an uncanny resemblance, although older, to those of his younger sister, Janey. This time he was not going to distance himself from the trouble. This time he would join in the attempt to reclaim a town.

Kane thought about Frank Crockett as he wandered down the dark street toward the livery. He had yet to get himself a clear look at Crockett. Pike, on the other hand, was always in evidence. He appeared to be making it his personal business to keep a close watch on the peddler. Kane kept a wary eye but gave the pretense of ignoring him.

Kane's boots rang soundly on the small sections of boardwalk the town boasted as he considered Crockett. The name wasn't familiar, but it wasn't necessarily his real one. Plenty of men took a new handle to drop out of sight, go unnoticed, or hide from the law. He would talk to Brown about that. He grinned to himself. After all, some men even cultivated ratty beards and shaggy hair and drove a peddler's wagon to avoid attention.

Since his arrival Kane had spotted a number of faces that were familiar to him. Joe Sparks he recognized from a run-in they'd had in Cold Flats. Sparks should have been dead or in jail by this time, but he was here. Sparks was someone Saquarra did not deserve and would do better without. It would do better without most of the *hombres* hanging around the streets at this time of night.

He entered the livery, closing the door behind him, leaving the darkness in favor of a pale, flickering light cast by a single coal-oil lamp burning half way down the length of the building. It was late, but Kane had learned the hosteler made a habit of leaving a lamp burning low in case one of Saquarra's visitors decided to ride out unannounced and unexpectedly.

The trail of a peddler was often a hazardous one, and Kane's many years on that trail had made him cautious, overly alert. The small hairs at the nape of his neck prickled. There was something here — someone.

Most of Kane's gear was stored in the stall alongside Buck, including the saddle he normally carried in the back of his wagon. The wagon had been left out behind the livery's corral, and, each time Kane checked it, he had found the contents exactly as they should be. For a town populated as Saquarra was with a continuous stream of outlaws and bandits, flowing through from both sides of the border, the only explanation was that Crockett was able to enforce a hands-off policy. A warning was implicit — anyone caught breaking Crockett's laws would be dealt with swiftly and severely. So Kane's merchandise was safe.

Kane paused. It wasn't the hosteler. He never stayed late according to the locals. Kane drew a deep breath and walked toward Buck's stall. He heard an odd rustling sound, one not common to a livery stable. But vying more urgently for his attention was a scrape and a thud overhead, muted by the sounds of crackling hay. If this was an ambush, it would not have Crockett's blessing. Someone was prepared to take a big risk, and Kane would be willing to bet it was Mississippi Pike. Kane kept moving and stepped up to Buck's stall, speaking softly to the blood-bay gelding.

"Easy Buck," he murmured to the horse in the ominous quiet of the stable. "Easy boy, it's just me."

Shuffling his hoofs in the straw of his bedding, Buck shook his head and snorted in recognition. He was uneasy, shifting from side to side, reaffirming another presence inside the livery.

As usual, Kane had not taken his rifle with him. It was in the compartment beneath the driver's box on the wagon. His six-gun was stashed with the gear near the back of Buck's stall and not very accessible. He was unarmed. *Fool,* he admonished himself. The flesh tingled along the back of Kane's neck. A stir of movement. The pale light of the coal-oil lamp flickered gently, then resumed its steady burn. The whisper of sound. The play of a dark shadow against the darker background. The obscurity outside the pool of soft, dim light was almost complete, the loft overhead black as a cave.

Kane hesitated, golden eyes sweeping the darkness. His ears sifted through the sounds, subtle and soft, searching for the warning he knew to lie beneath the silence. He stayed where he was for an instant, watching Buck's ears flick back and forth nervously, then he continued on toward the back of the livery.

Overhead a soft scuffing noise pricked his senses, a pause echoed before a sharp whisper of sound sent Kane diving for cover. A gunshot had cracked within the stable's walls. Lightning reflexes took over; his response was instantaneous. He crashed onto the straw-laden floor, rolling for the sparse cover the planks dividing the stalls would provide.

Kane's heart thundered in his ears. Only a few inches' difference and he wouldn't have been considering his next move. Blood heated and surged in his veins. He wormed his way farther into the stall. His adrenaline was up, but there was no way to release it. He had no gun, no knife.

The gunshot had come from overhead in the loft. Then he remembered the rustling he had heard below.

He had to consider that it might be Samantha. Just at the moment he had decided to make a dash for his gun in Buck's stall, he heard the sharp, cackling laugh he had come to recognize over the past few days.

"Hey, peddler," Mississippi Pike called maliciously from above, "bet you never moved that fast in your life. I'm gonna give you a chance to try it again."

Kane remained still. For the moment he knew he was out of Pike's sight. He waited, his heart thumping with a heavy, measured beat. He ached to move. He barely breathed. He had time enough to wonder what the hell he was doing in this place, this town, when a low, hushed whisper snapped at him. It was the last thing he had expected.

"Here, catch!" The two words barely gave him warning. His six-gun pinwheeled over the side of Buck's stall, glinting in the dim light of the lamp for just an instant. His hand shot out to grab it. He was into a dive when the butt of the gun slapped his palm. He began to roll, tipping the gun barrel toward the loft floor. He was sprawled and braced when his finger took up the slack on the trigger. He loosed four slugs in rapid succession, the roar of the gun numbing the air as he traced from memory Pike's path above. The acrid smell of gun powder was strong as he rolled clear.

There was a mad scrambling in the loft overhead, but Kane doubted he had hit anything.

Silence settled in the livery once again. Kane held his breath, no longer fearing attack from another quarter, having determined that Samantha had thrown him his gun. Now there was only Pike.

The drygulcher's voice drifted from farther back along the wall. "Tell you what, you get yourself on out of town fast enough, and I reckon I'll just let you go."

Pike's footsteps moved swiftly through scattered straw in the loft until silence returned in the wake of his words with startling abruptness. Only the low, agitated snorts and shufflings of disturbed horses remained.

Kane's breath sang between his teeth as he let his breath out in a long, low whistle, not quite ready to release the tension coiled in his body. The clamor of his fighting blood urged him to go after Mississippi, but good sense held him back.

The gentle *swoosh* of skirts across the wooden, straw-strewn floor brought Kane to one knee as Samantha stepped out from the next stall. She looked down at him and gnawed at her lip.

Kane started at the sound of running outside the stable.

"What's going on in here?" came the sound of Sheriff Brown's voice, as his head peaked around the threshold of the door.

Kane stepped forward at the same time Samantha leaped back into the shadows. "Oh, Sheriff, I'm sorry about the commotion," Kane explained. "I thought I saw a rattler in here when I was checking my horse. Anyway, it sure looked like a snake to me."

"You'd better be more careful," Brown responded, a puzzled look on his face. "In this town it's best not to go off shooting."

"I know that, Sheriff. I guess I'm just a bit jumpy. It won't happen again."

"All right, good night." As he turned to leave the sheriff added: "I told you to watch your back."

Once Brown left, Kane and Samantha remained silent for several moments.

"He could have killed you," she finally commented.

Kane gave her a grin. "Doubtful," he stated, "but he might have heard you moving around in here. I know I did. Heard your skirts rustlin'."

Samantha momentarily paled. "He . . . he couldn't have. He was above us in the loft."

Kane lifted his shoulder and looked unconvinced. "Whatever you say."

"If you're trying to scare me, you're doing a pretty good job of it."

"Lady, I think you've got plenty good reason to be scared already without my tryin' to add to it." He brushed off bits of straw that had collected on his clothing. He smiled to himself to release some of the stress of the past few minutes. Old feelings, memories of that terribly young, all-but-forgotten soldier he had been stirred within him.

Samantha read his expression all wrong. "This is funny to you, isn't it? Just a big game. Why can't you just leave?" She wanted to add — *And take me with you!* — but didn't.

"I have business here, and my horse needs a breather from the trail. I'm more curious as to what you're doing here and why you tossed me my gun."

"You've done business here. You should get out of Saquarra before it's too late. What will it take to make you see that?"

70

He smiled wickedly at her. "A beautiful woman's concern is usually enough, but you didn't answer my question."

"I owed you for helping me. Besides, now you know all of Saquarra's dirty little secrets, mine included. I want to go with you when you leave town."

He shook his head. "Haven't you heard the rumor? I'm not leaving. I plan on staying for a while."

"You're what . . . ? Why on God's earth would you want to stay here?"

"Fiddlefoot just up an' died on me, I reckon. I've had a look around. I've even talked to Zeb over at the general store about buying him out and expanding the business . . . although I'd move it mid-way between here and Mex-town."

Samantha stiffened, her demeanor as cold as a Montana winter. Her chin rose, and her eyes became guarded. "I know the good folks of this town. If you think they're going to do their buying where those . . . those people do theirs, then you've got a lot to learn."

"Probably so," Kane admitted, "but, since I'd be the proprietor of the only general store and trading post in the area for miles, I suspect the 'good people,' as you call them, would be doing some learning right along with me."

He stepped around the divider into Buck's stall. There he squatted down beside his gear and retrieved his holster. He rose, draping it over a wooden slat while he reloaded his gun. He spun the barrel, feeling the smoothness of the motion, snugged steel into leather, and slung it about his hips, buckling it down. If

Crockett's policies weren't going to protect him against Pike, he had better be ready.

Samantha stared at him. She shifted nervously which made her skirts rustle softly. His revelation was unsettling. She had not heard that he intended to stay on in Saquarra. But then she didn't hear much, since her presence nearly anywhere tended to produce a hushed silence except in the saloon. Moreover, Mississippi kept close watch over her these days, and she spent most of her time in her room.

She felt the lump lodge in her throat, the first sign of imminent tears, tears she did not wish to shed in front of Kane. Things had never seemed right for her since the war. In its aftermath she had left Virginia, heading west to find a position as a schoolteacher. She had never stayed long in one place, never understanding herself why she could not settle down. Then she was kidnapped, dragged off, and brought here. She knew her brother would believe her dead by now and that thought, after all they had lost, broke her heart. She had to get away from Saquarra.

The words were brimming in her throat, the plea locked behind her teeth, ready to spill over when the door at the front of the livery swung open again. Kane spun, gun in right hand, half crouched. In that instant his lean, angular face took on the stone-like appearance Samantha had so frequently seen on the itinerants passing through.

Kane's gorge of recently aroused fury rose but was quickly tamped down as Ben Ford, the stout, rumpled owner of the livery, entered with a lively step. His black, button eyes darted around the livery's interior then came to rest on Kane, standing upright, gun in hand. Ben stood frozen with a startled look on his face.

"Everythin' all right?" the short, broad-shouldered man asked. "I heard some shootin'."

"Shouldn't it be?" Kane eased off.

Ben shrugged his nervous uncertainty, but his reply was blunt. "I was leavin' the saloon when I seen you come in here. Then I heard the shots and next I seen Mississippi come out. Knowin' the way you and Pike started off t'other day, I just figured there mighta been some trouble. I got my business to think of." Undecided as to how much he should say, he paused. "That Mississippi is a bad'n to tangle with. Has a foul temper. Any man in Saquarra could tell you as much."

"You told me . . . ," Kane probed, feeling out the other man's attitude regarding Saquarra and the type of trade it was attracting.

Suddenly Ford looked wary. "Don't go makin' nothin' outa that. You got some advice a couple of days ago to get your tail clear of Saquarra before you got it caught in a crack, and, the way it looks to me, that was damn' good advice. Still is. You want, I'll help you hitch up right now."

Samantha stepped forward, the crisp crinkle of her taffeta skirts drawing the attention of the two men.

The movement forced Ben to acknowledge her presence, nodding at her. He said nothing, but his gaze moved slowly back and forth between Kane and Samantha, reading significance in their being here together. He hunched his shoulders and jammed his

73

hands into his pockets. "Oh, Miss Samantha, this ain't good, this ain't good a-tall," Ben said finally, shaking his head. His gaze shifted to Kane. "Mister," he said solemnly, "you're really hunting it."

Kane left the livery. Ben Ford and the rest of the prominent citizens of Saquarra would be finding out soon enough exactly how much he was hunting it.

CHAPTER
SEVEN

Things often look different with the coming of a new day. But, as far as Samantha was concerned, things looked the same. The bright, sun-splashed dawn of a new day had brought little to cheer her. She paced in her room, feeling caged like an animal. She retraced the same path over and over again, pausing occasionally by the side window on the second floor to glance out on the street below. At this time in the morning Saquarra looked like any ordinary town. Quiet and peaceful. She was about to turn away from the window when she saw Kane coming down the street. Today he was going well-heeled. The newly added hardware was not a surprising sight in light of Mississippi's attack of the night before.

What came as a surprise to the others out on the street was the fact that he was still here. His wagon had been spotted, hitched up and ready to roll out around dawn. Word had spread quickly.

Samantha studied Kane. He seemed somehow to look differently this morning. She examined him more closely. It was in the way he moved, the way he held himself. Something was different in this man from the one who had first rolled into town. He moved with a looser gait and wore an alert look. His head turned constantly, taking in all there was to see. He exuded a confidence and surety that only the likes of Crockett displayed on the streets of Saquarra.

She continued to keep an eye on him as he strolled the length of the dusty street, heading straight for Mex-town. He nodded to the passers-by on foot and horseback, acknowledging the presence of everyone on the street. *What drove a man like Kane?* she wondered.

The window was only open slightly, but she could hear his words of greeting drift up from the street. She could smell the hot dust and the aroma of horses. Her attention was drawn by a few Mexican children, laughing and running back and forth across the street. It was a quiet scene, really, one she could have enjoyed in the not-so-distant past — children running and playing, laughing and teasing each other. She had a fondness for children, but like a dash of cold water she remembered where these particular children belonged. They came from Mex-town. The boys would grow into men like Manuel Avilar who had dragged her here, sold her like a slave, and left again to commit some other atrocity.

Before she had been kidnapped, she had never thought much about the Mexican people, but now she loathed them. They repulsed her. She was thankful that those who lived in Saquarra were relegated to their own side of town, all except for the slimy bandits who roamed at will. With those individuals she avoided even occupying the same side of the street.

She shuddered. Her hatred of all Mexicans was unwarranted. She couldn't really blame the children for the acts of a few men, but she did. She hated each and every one, big and small, young and old. They were no better than Apaches. She remembered the South and the cruelty of its system of slavery. She recalled the feeling of revulsion she had known when others had been repelled by dark skin. What she had never experienced in Virginia, she was experiencing now. She could not look at the people of Mex-town without seeing them as the enemy. The realization of this contradiction shook her.

For the first time in a long while she longed to return to Virginia to see her older brother, Brock. Perhaps things were better now. Maybe she wouldn't be the burden she would have been a couple of years ago. Surely she could find a teaching job somewhere there. In Virginia the circumstances of her life here could be well hidden.

She was distracted from her thoughts by the sudden sound of rapid hoofbeats. Her eyes swept up, then down, the main thoroughfare before she saw the horses and riders. It wasn't an uncommon sight in Saquarra, hoodlums racing their horses, dust flying from beneath the horses' hoofs, people and animals scattering before them. Except this time there were children playing in the street. Spread out across the barren street where it angled into Mex-town, they were oblivious as children always are when at play.

Samantha threw open the window without thought, screaming out a warning. "Look out! Get off the street!"

Even if they did not understand her words, Samantha's yell attracted the attention of several of the children, enough so that they looked up and understood the danger of the situation. They called at the others and raced for the adjacent buildings. One ducked behind a watering trough. Only one remained. A small boy, younger than the rest with straight shining black hair and a cherubic round face who stood paralyzed in the street.

"Run!" Samantha yelled out again, beating her fist on the window sill, praying the intentionally piercing note of her voice would jar the boy to action. "Run!"

The child remained as still as a statue. Out of the corner of her eye Samantha saw movement ahead of the racing horses. It was the peddler who had been half way up the street when Samantha first yelled. He was running for the stunned child. His speed was not nearly that of a racing horse, but he had a lead on them.

Samantha leaned out the window, gripping its edge. Her knuckles turned white, and she held her breath. Would he reach the boy in time? A little boy for whom only a few minutes before she had felt disdain because the color of his skin and his hair was the same as the men who had sold her into slavery of another sort. Her only wish was that Kane could reach the boy in time to save his life.

"Get out of the way!" Kane bellowed at the child, hoping the boy would be startled into moving on his own. Kane feared he couldn't make the boy move in time but was driven to try again. "Run! Move!"

The little boy turned his head in the direction of Kane's thundering voice but seemed unable to move from the spot where he sat now, crying.

Samantha bit her lip until she drew blood, as the peddler, in a loose-limbed dive, snagged the urchin, somehow wrapping himself around him as he rolled. There was very little she could see beyond a tangled sprawl, straining horses, and great gusts of dust and sand as the outlaws careened headlong and uncaring up the street.

Kane had the boy curled beneath him and was still rolling when the horses pounded through the lane. Somehow the animals managed to avoid crushing the two as they side-stepped past, the peddler collecting a couple of good kicks before they were just as suddenly gone.

Then all was stillness on the street. Kane began straightening out. Abruptly, it seemed, the street became alive with activity. A woman, who could only be the boy's mother, raced toward the child, arms extended, her wails of fear filling the air.

Samantha waited tensely, watching. Kane climbed to his feet and propped the boy up on his own. She could see him leaning down to talk to the boy before his mother scooped him up, babbling her gratitude in Spanish to the peddler.

Kane turned and looked up in Samantha's direction. He grinned and gave a short wave. At the same time the door to her room swung open behind her. Pike was across the room before she could move away from the window. He looked down on the street below and angrily backhanded her across the face which sent her reeling to the floor. "I told you, I don't want you even lookin' at him!"

"I wasn't!" Samantha lied, her hand going to her bruised cheek, where a new imprint, starkly white against the redness of her sunburn, stood out in harsh relief. The raw sting brought tears of pain to her eyes as she dabbed a finger at the trickle of blood dribbling from the corner of her mouth.

Pike turned from her, glaring out the window, leaving Samantha to pick herself up off the floor. She did it gingerly, wary that he might hit her again. Despite her fear she allowed some of her anger to show.

"There's a lot more down there on that street besides some damned peddler you can't get off your mind."

Mercurial as always, Pike stood watching Kane's figure move up the street, grinning. "Peddler's playin' with the Mex kids, but I see he got hisself some hardware. That's good. It'll make killin' him more fun."

Anger continued to mount within Samantha's breast, making it difficult even to draw a breath. She must curb it. Kane was her best chance of getting away from Mississippi and this hell-hole of a town. She must not arouse Mississippi's suspicion. She had to convince Zachariah Kane to help her.

"You want to see him die, sweetheart?" Pike directed the scathing question at her.

Samantha's answer was to move farther across the room. Kane might be only a peddler, and, although he was thinking of settling in Saquarra, Samantha was

80

determined to see him leave — alive and with her in his wagon

Kane was shaken by his encounter with the hoofs of those flying horses. He had not incurred any severe injuries, although several times the hoofs had made contact with some powerful kicks. He would probably have some ugly bruises in the morning. He was dusting himself off, when, as he glanced up, he saw Samantha leaning on the sill of her window. He waved — a gesture he hoped would let her know he was all right. He watched as a figure appeared behind her and, then, Pike took Samantha's place at the window. Upon seeing Kane, his face did not register relief as had Samantha's. Instead, Pike grimaced and then turned away from the window in a flash. Kane saw Pike raise his arm, and then he was out of range from the window. Everything in Kane urged him to run up to Samantha's room and beat Pike within an inch of his life. He had to restrain himself. *Damn that Pike!* He filled Kane with a fear for Samantha.

Fear can be accompanied by any number of odd sensations. It can propel a man forward or freeze him with anxiety. Or, it can leave him standing in the middle of a dusty street, feeling helpless and dark with fury. During that last, soul-shattering year of the war there had been those who claimed the heart of young Kane was a pit of coal blackness. Perhaps that much was true, for how did a man separate what he had been from what he had become? Did a man ever really change or merely show another face to the world? And, if change it truly was, was there room for change again? Kane believed his darkness back then had been more of an eclipse of the heart than a blackness of the soul. But then, that was what he *wanted* to believe. And, in this belief, he found justification for what he was about to do, and solace for the pain of the past.

Last night, after his second run-in with Pike, Kane had decided that settling in Saquarra had been a bad idea from the start. When a man made mistakes, he had to rectify them. He would leave the next morning just as soon as he picked up a few staples — flour and coffee — from the general store. The wagon had been hitched up accordingly. But in the time it took to draw a breath, all that had changed — again. The feel of that boy in his arms, all sharp bones and angles as they had tumbled across the street together, had brought it all back. Jesus, the children. All through another war the children had suffered. They had lain dead in the roads and fields. They had donned uniforms at an age when they should have been catching frogs in a creek. They had been slaughtered in battle with nothing but a drum in their hands. Seeing that small boy in the street about to be pounded to a pulp beneath the horses' hoofs had brought it all back with a vengeance. It had given him the shakes. A cold knot lay in his stomach, threatening to uncurl like a steel blade. It was the young and defenseless who suffered the most. And it was they who would not be protected, not unless the root cause was eradicated. This town desperately needed to help itself, but it lacked direction. He might be able to give it that.

Kane was now packing a gun, strapped to his hip, a rifle caught up in his hand. He scrubbed a hand over the street-dusted, black, unkempt beard that darkened and obscured his face, giving him the appearance of a bristling stray dog, and headed over to Sheriff Brown's office. A few of the good citizens of Saquarra had provided him more than passing appraisal. Gossip would spread like the wash of the morning sun.

"Think maybe we have to have a talk," Kane said as he closed the door behind him.

Clive Brown let his feet slip from the corner of the desk where they had been propped, his bootheels ringing against the wooden floor as he came upright in his chair, laying aside the papers he had been reading.

Kane dropped into the chair in front of the sheriff's desk, positioning his rifle beside his knee.

The lawman stood up, taking a blue-speckled metal cup from a hook and strode over to the stove. There he hefted a squat, dented coffee pot. He had figured this to be coming, but he didn't have to be pleased by it. After all, Saquarra really wasn't this man's fight. Now, the sheriff figured, he was going to do the smart thing and pull his freight.

"Coffee?" he asked, lifting the cup in Kane's general direction.

Kane nodded, and the sheriff poured the brew, thick and black into the cup, and handed it over to him. Then he refilled his own and returned to the desk to hitch a hip over the edge, half leaning, half sitting, regarding the peddler over the top of his steaming coffee.

Old habit kept the hot cup of Joe in Kane's left hand. As if he could read it, he knew what was on the sheriff's mind. A slow smile spread across his face.

"Everything work out okay last night?" the sheriff offered as an opening.

"Nobody got hurt. Even that snake."

"He'll come at you again." Brown looked at him intently, waiting, trying to sift through the peddler's mind. "What you just did out there on the street won't endear you to his heart none neither."

"Sheriff," Kane asked bluntly, "what do you want to do about this town?"

The coffee slid down Clive Brown's throat like a solid lump. "You thinkin' the two of us . . . ?"

Kane nodded, tipping his cup to his lips, and waited.

The sheriff stood up, in agitation brushing coffee droplets from his mustache with the back of his hand. He had been prepared for almost anything but this. Hell, he'd thought the peddler was going to announce he was leaving. "What you're proposin' could end with both of us shakin' hands with Saint Peter."

Kane grinned, unperturbed. "You've got trouble brewin' here, Sheriff. I don't think there's any avoiding it. There're good people in this town, and they're scared. I thought just a while ago that I could ride out, leave it behind, but I just found out I can't. It would just stick in my craw to do that. I don't see you pullin' up stakes, neither. If we come at this thing together, maybe we'll get lucky and find some more help. In fact, I'm counting on that, and then we might stand a chance. If we wait for it to come to us, we won't survive it. If we want to stay above snakes, we're gonna have to take a stand."

"I want this town cleaned up," Brown said, frowning, "but I aim to keep my own hide whole in the process. And I have the citizens of Saquarra to think of, too." He tried another gulp of the steaming liquid, welcoming the hot, bitter taste. "I stayed on here as sheriff because I hoped I could do something, but I didn't figure to brace 'em alone. I don't know, son, but what you're askin' is over my head."

Kane looked Brown squarely in the face. "You're not alone any more. And you're not an old man ready for a rocker."

Kane felt like an old man himself. He was exhausted, more tired than he had ever felt before his life, even during the long, grueling nights on the battlefield when he had feared sleep. This was a different sort of depletion. And, surfacing in a rush, was the long-buried desire to shed somehow the pain of the past. To stop drifting and make a life for himself. He drew a deep breath and let it out slowly. That was what had been niggling at him when he had first thought to settle here, before he had realized just how bad it was.

"I'm sorry, Sheriff, but, once the dance starts, I don't think you're going to have any choice but to join in."

"Man makes his choices."

"Not all the time. Sometimes it's thrust on him. Look at Samantha Cameron."

Kane set his empty tin cup aside with a hollow clunk before hefting his rifle and rising to his feet. Sheriff Brown backed off a step as the peddler rose.

"You still look doubtful, Clive." Kane's voice had lost its edge, the words now blunted. He walked to the door. "If I'm forced to do it alone, I will." He rested his hand a moment on the door latch. "I want your help. You think about it for a spell, but you best know the dance is about to begin."

Kane closed the door behind him.

Frank Crockett stood at the end of the bar, an attractive man, sun-browned. He wore his sandy-colored hair long over his shoulders and his neatly-trimmed mustache waxed. He was relaxed and appeared unconcerned, yet there was little that escaped his attention as he sipped his beer. His ear cocked toward the man next to him who was bending it.

"You'd think Pike was a plannin' on marryin' that li'l gal the way he took on an' went after that peddler fella." Roary Sikes snickered, droplets of beer and flecks of foam spraying from his thick lips. "Hell, even when he brung her into town all torn up and smellin' to high heaven, ol' Mississippi had a look on his face like he'd died an' gone to heaven. He's gone plumb loco. Tried to shoot that peddler last night, I hear." He took another great gulp of beer.

Frank regarded him from distinctive amber eyes. "That a fact?" he asked with deceptive calm.

"Surely is."

"Well, the peddler's not dead. Neither is Pike."

"Surprisin', ain't it?"

"More than that. A whole lot more."

Roary plunked his heavy beer glass down on the bar. "Looks to some like Mississippi might be gettin' too big for his britches and takin' on a chaw too big for him to wrap his teeth around. You find yourself lookin' for a new *segundo,* give me a holler."

Roary Sikes was a greasy drifter from whom it was much better to remain down wind. Still, the fact remained, and Crockett turned it over in his mind time and again. Something would have to be done about Mississippi Pike, and it would have to be done soon.

Sikes straightened from the bar, a short, square man wearing a pair of pistols tucked in the waistband of his filthy pants. "Just you keep me in mind when the time comes," he said, then short-stepped his way from the saloon, boots beating an uneven tattoo.

Crockett frowned a little when he half turned to find Buck Mitchell, one of the biggest ranchers in the area, staring at him over the top of a whiskey glass. The town boss shot the rancher a look meant to quell insurrection, but Mitchell just summoned a rascally smile and tossed back the drink.

"Havin' some trouble keepin' it clear just who the hell's runnin' things hereabouts?" he asked. He thumped the whiskey glass down on the bar and called over his shoulder to the bartender: "Gimme another one."

"No concern of yours," Crockett returned sharply.

"No, none a-tall. I don't much care what goes on here as long as my boys have a place where they can come to raise a little ruckus and where the wife can pay a visit to the general store now and then. Still, there are some things a man might be forced to take a hand in."

"You don't want to go messing with a hornet's nest, Buck."

"Naw, I surely don't. But don't you neither get to thinking me and my outfit's all gurgle and no guts an' that nobody jaggled my arm when the good Lord poured in the brains. That *segundo* of yours is makin' people nervous on both sides of the deadline, and that means folks are questioning your ability."

The bartender sloshed Buck a refill. The rancher lifted it to his lips, tossing it back without a second's hesitation.

"Nothing's changed recently on that score," Crockett growled. "My men do what I say. As for the rest, they do the same or they find the desert mighty quick."

Buck pushed himself away from the bar, shoving his dusty brown hat back on his head. "Hell, Crockett," he grumbled, "I'm with you . . . just as long as the town stays quiet. I got a ranch to run. Don't have time for no hell-hole what's just as likely to dry up an' blow away some day as a flower in an east wind. Just take a look around this town. Hell, when the silver mine busted, what'd the folks around here do? They went and toted all that extra timber on down and used it to put up buildings. Said it was better than usin' adobe an' havin' the dirt sifting down in their soup all the time. Don't have the sense God gave a gnat. All their places are hot in the summer and drafty in the winter. And they're dry as tinder." Buck shook his head in disbelief. "I best be gettin' on. See you around, Frank."

Crockett watched as the batwings swung shut behind Buck and pondered the situation. Back in the beginning the rancher's attitude had given Crockett the power of a benevolent god over Saquarra. Buck Mitchell was the barometer by which to gauge the thinking going on around town. And Buck Mitchell didn't seem any too happy with the climate these days. Crockett stared into the quiet, amber surface of his beer, and it occurred to him to wonder from what cloth the peddler was cut.

Word had spread that the peddler was leaving; then he didn't. Crockett had heard he had pulled a kid from out in front of stampeding horses. That alone took a lot of sand if the man had more than pudding for brains. And Mississippi had braced the hawker once more, against his orders, coming out short of his goal. The peddler might just prove to be the answer to the dilemma Crockett faced regarding Pike. He would shoot the man himself if need be, but he much preferred the more round-about approach. His *segundo* was a bulldog when he had his mind set. If Zachariah Kane was a match for him . . . well, it was worth thinking about.

CHAPTER
EIGHT

"Hey, will you lookee thar' boys, look who's come to walk among us!" Mississippi crowed over his drink loud enough for half the town to hear. "It's the tin-pan man."

Kane entered the coolness of the saloon's interior, leaving the blazing afternoon sun behind. His eyes swept the place with an appraising glance.

Pike downed his drink in one gulp and wiped the back of his hand across his lips as he set his glass back on the bar for a refill. A ripple of laughter crossed the room and died in chilled silence. Pike smirked. He was working his way up to a roaring drunk.

"Oh, oh, boys, he's packin' now! Must've heard what a hard town this is."

Kane watched the bartender, a tall, spare man whose only real bulk seemed centered in his forearms. He hovered near Pike and poured another generous drink into Pike's glass and cast a wary glance in almost every direction. And with good cause from what Kane could see as he ventured farther into the room, holster riding snugged down at his hip, rifle hanging loosely from his hand.

Mississippi kept his eyes glued on the peddler, and Kane, eyes flat and cold, met the *segundo*'s challenging regard with lips thinned down and jaw set. He squashed an urge to backhand Pike's grinning face and take him apart right then and there. Crockett's second in command, for all his petty, back-stabbing, murderous inclinations, was not his primary concern, not at this moment. Frank Crockett was.

Kane could not help but see the stern look of warning as it passed from Crockett's amber eyes to Pike, who pretended not to notice. Nonetheless, he fell silent suddenly and turned his attention to the drink the uncomfortable bartender had placed on the bar before him. The sneer on his lips and the venomous look in his eyes were still blatant. It would not be long before the big man's *segundo* made a grab for the top job. When that happened, someone was going to die.

Crockett turned to sweep Kane with his steady gaze. There was something there. An appraisal, a weighing. One more glance at the peddler and his eyes dropped back to the game of solitaire spread before him on the table where he was sitting.

Kane, in turn, studied Crockett. As a peddler Kane was a good judge of men, and he knew he was not mistaken in his evaluation of Saquarra's head man. He was calculating and dangerous.

"Beer," Kane said softly to the bartender, once he had strode across the room, propping his rifle near his knee.

This was the first time he had actually seen the head man close up. The war had taught him many things —

things which he had not forgotten over the years. The primary lesson he had learned was to know your adversary but not to give your adversary the same advantage. He had also learned to have a plan of action.

Collecting the tall, brimming glass of beer before him, Kane lifted his rifle and sought out a table in a far, dim corner. He sat down with his back to the wall, once again leaning the familiar weapon against his knee. From beneath the lowered brim of his hat he gave Crockett intense scrutiny. Mississippi Pike, the heel of his finely tooled boot hooked over the brass rail running along the floor in front of the bar, was giving Kane the same close study he was giving Crockett.

"Got me shakin' in my boots, just seein' him totin' iron," Pike murmured to his nearest companion who obliged with an amiable chuckle.

Kane sipped his drink and ignored Pike. Instead, his eyes moved around the saloon, always returning to Crockett at the table near the window overlooking the street. The man appeared cool and undisturbed as a meandering mountain stream. He wore no jacket or vest over his white shirt with an open collar and turned-back cuffs. His face was darkly tanned with a neatly trimmed, waxed mustache shading his upper lip. He had broad, well-muscled shoulders, the kind a man got from working timber country, digging in a mine, or maybe handling a team of six or eight mules or horses for a time. Heavy eyebrows gave his face a commanding presence, a dominance that the men who rode with him read as strength. The enormity of the power the man craved showed in the set of his face. The power he already possessed was amply displayed in the way he controlled the room with only a glance or slight movement. They might grumble, cuss, and get a bit rowdy, but none there was likely to step over Crockett's boundaries. Not yet.

Impregnability was the key to Frank Crockett. Take that away and he would crumble. Take away Crockett and the whole set up in Saquarra would follow suit. With any luck the place might be fit to live in again. And the tin-pan man had a plan.

Kane drank his beer, foam catching on his face hair and framing his mouth before he dashed the dense cluster of bubbles with the back of his hand, then absently caressed the damp hair into place. His eyes swept the room again in another quick appraisal, then shifted back to Crockett. He thought it would be interesting to observe Saquarra's head man be forced to draw the gun hanging so unimposingly from his hip. It never hurt to see the man you were up against draw. But such an event was unlikely. Kane put his mind to his evolving plan as he nursed his brew. The sheriff walked in.

Brown stopped just inside the door. His eyes took in everything and everyone in the saloon until they came to rest on Kane. Then, with long, purposeful strides, he crossed the room and pulled up a chair across from him. That was enough to drag Kane's attention from Crockett, and he did not like it. He doubted Saquarra's big man would appreciate the sheriff's spending time with a peddler — especially one of whom it was becoming common knowledge that he was gnatting about town like a fly hangs around dung. But Crockett glanced only briefly in the sheriff's direction, then ignored him. Brown was obviously not worth his trouble. That was a big mistake in judgment from the peddler's viewpoint.

"Something you wanted to see me about, Sheriff?" Kane spoke in a low monotone across the top of his beer glass. "If so, you reckon this here's the best place for it?"

"Forget about Crockett," Brown growled. "He thinks I'm trying to move you on. He thinks I don't like peddlers."

"Uhn huh. Nice to be so sure of yourself since you ain't exactly workin' from a base of strength," said Kane, giving Brown a little rub, his golden eyes flickering past the sheriff occasionally to light on Pike where he still stood, his back to the bar, elbows propped on the wood, glowering back at him. "So," Kane prodded, "what's your problem?"

"Ain't mine as much as it's yours."

"Mine?" Kane's lips lifted at the corners and stared straight at Pike. He watched as the owner of the town's only gun shop stepped up to the bar beside him.

"You're walkin' armed. It's makin' this whole damn' town edgy. Word is you've been doin' a whole lot of talking to a whole bunch of folks since you left my office. You're stirrin' up the people in Saquarra real good."

"Yep."

"Could take it a mite more easy."

"It's my neck, and I'll risk it the way *I* see fit." Kane waved his glass in the direction of the bar. "You better do something, Sheriff," he said easily, "because one of our good citizens is looking to get himself killed." Appearing unconcerned, he took another pull on his beer.

"What!?" Sheriff Brown glanced toward the bar, instantly spotting the cause for concern. Red Grissom, the local gunsmith, was half of the trouble, and, as usual, the other half was Mississippi Pike. Crockett's *segundo* had had too much to drink, not that he needed alcohol as an excuse. Grissom, apparently a little drunk already before he entered this saloon, brushed shoulders with Pike at the bar, and Pike had flared instantly. Unruffled, Red moved, but Pike was crowding him now, and, while the gunsmith was not the kind of man to start something, neither was he the kind to back down from it once it was started. Not even if trouble was brewing with a man like Mississippi Pike.

Kane saw it in the way the shopkeeper held himself that he was stupidly anticipating a fist fight. Pike had other ideas. His hand was drifting toward the knife hilt protruding from his belt sheath when the sheriff stepped between them, grabbed Grissom by the shirt front, and dragged him out the saloon door.

Frank Crockett had suspended play on his hand of solitaire, fastening his steady gaze on his second in command as Saquarra's sheriff hustled the gunsmith out the door. He did not say a word, but his expression made plain his feelings on the matter. Cold anger was etched in the lines of his face.

Pike grinned, tossing down another drink, swaying a little, blithely unaware of the stony cast of Crockett's amber eyes. Either that or he did not care. If he didn't care, Crockett would have to move soon.

Kane watched Crockett and Pike. If he took out Crockett before Crockett could take out Pike . . . ? If he could get the sheriff to go along, it just might work. He watched Pike intently.

In his hand Pike now held a knife equipped with a blade a good six inches in length. He stood, fondling its razor sharp edge as he half turned, leering openly in Kane's direction.

"Sheeet! If these boys ain't just a-huntin' it tonight. I mean, I was just funnin' when I said I was scairt, but maybe they don't know that. Mebbe I got to show 'em."

Fury deepened the color in Crockett's eyes as they rested on his top man. Mississippi was fast becoming a threat to the security of Saquarra, the kingdom Frank Crockett had nurtured so carefully.

Kane saw the almost imperceptible drop of Crockett's hand toward the gun that rode at his hip.

"Think maybe you've had enough, Mississippi," The voice was mellow, the razor-edged words a sharp command.

Kane stiffened and set his beer glass down. *Not yet,* Kane thought to himself. *Just a little longer.* This not being something he had any intention of interfering in, he waited, enveloped by the tension curling through the saloon like smoke caught on a draft. From his position at the bar Pike could not see Crockett's gun or the long-fingered hand that curled around the smooth butt. The peddler had a better vantage point. He had a clear view of the unfolding drama. And he was not about to trust entirely to Crockett's authority. He lifted his rifle across his lap.

A raw, rasping chuckle grated from Pike's throat, and he reveled in the many pairs of eyes upon him, turning back to the bar for another drink. His knife, finely honed, shone like silver in the saloon's pale light.

Crockett seethed, but his face remained still. He was testing Pike, pressing him to see how far his authority still extended over the man. He could pull the trigger on his *segundo* right now, if he felt it necessary, and he wasn't even raising a sweat over it. He gauged the hunch of the man's shoulders, the tension taut in that whipcord body. He had long since made a friend of the burning knot which lurked in his stomach in moments of disquiet. It gave him no pause while he continued his appraisal of Pike, gun butt pressing against his palm.

"Whatever you say, boss!" Pike finally slurred in loud jocularity. He slammed back another drink, slid the knife clumsily back into its sheath, blade drawing blood from a carelessly placed thumb, and staggered for the door.

Crockett eased off, turning back to his cards, but not before sweeping Kane with another measuring glance. The look of cunning in his eyes when they rested upon him gave Kane additional food for thought.

With the tense moment past, the saloon returned to its usual raucous volume as the flow of customers increased with the approach of sunset. Kane remained where he was, relaxed and starting to work on his second beer. He watched men come and go, though few seemed to go, and more kept coming. He recognized more faces than he cared to. A peddler had a way of getting around, of seeing things, and of remembering. Some of the faces he saw graced wanted fliers; some he recognized from descriptions relayed to him on his travels. Then there was the man who just entered through the batwings, a man he remembered from his own past.

Joe Sparks. A dried-up, coarse, reptile of a man with eyes dark and cold as the moon in the night sky. He had seen him before in town. Kane had crossed trails with him a couple of years earlier. He watched him now from half-closed eyes, feeling the heat of the man's attention directed toward him as he, too, remembered.

He could still see Sparks in his mind's eye clear as anything, just as he had that day long past. Sparks, his cousin at his elbow, their bunch strung out behind, had descended upon the hapless town where Kane had been selling some household goods. A party to more hell-raising and killing than stealing, they had swept into the dusty, uneven street with guns blazing. A gun battle had been the last thing on Kane's mind when he had rolled into that town of Cold Flats. He had been staring right into Sparks's eyes after a blast from Kane's rifle had taken out the man's cousin with resounding finality. The rest of the town had piled in after that, guns blazing, and Sparks had found himself suddenly running for his life.

He was looking at Kane now like he was unfinished business. The promise of vengeance glinted from the depths of his eyes.

Outside, the sun had set, enveloping the streets of Saquarra in darkness. Kane continued to watch the renegade. The outlaw gave nothing away. Occasionally he glanced in Kane's direction, but his eyes never lingered long, and the expression on his craggy face never changed.

Kane watched closely as well, and, while it apparently was evident to no one else, it was plain to him. Joe Sparks was not drinking. He was making a show of it, but he had actually downed only one drink since he had entered the saloon and first clasped eyes on him. Trouble was brewing. Kane could smell it on the wind.

He set what was left of his second beer on the table, thoughtfully licking his lips as he climbed to his feet and leisurely started toward the batwings. Then, eyes resting on the Bowie sheathed at Sparks's waist, Kane remembered that after leaving Cold Flats he had heard that Sparks was a knife man. He was a man who could wield it or throw it, and he just loved to gut-stick a man.

It was an odd feeling which assailed Kane as he stepped out the door. It was anticipation vibrating with the resonance of a tuning fork. He knew just as surely as the sun was coming up in the morning that Sparks would be right on his heels. Kane would be ready for him.

A Mexican lounged in a chair tipped back on two legs, watching Kane intently. Hell, everybody in this town seemed to be watching somebody else. Freshly bathed and well turned-out in clean clothes obviously recently shut of their trail dust, the Mexican met Kane's eyes directly, grinning broadly as the peddler stepped out through the batwings into the night.

CHAPTER
NINE

The batwings whipped closed behind him, and Kane turned south, cat-footing it along the line of Saquarra's many false-fronted buildings. He felt a warning prickle raise the hairs along the back of his neck as heavy footsteps rang on wood, then thudded into dust close behind him. Sparks, just as anticipated. But there was more to think about. There was the Mexican. He did not know the man. Only one set of footsteps sounded behind him, but he would remember the Mexican.

More than once, when he had fought for the Union, Kane had been through this end of the spyglass and knew it would end with either him or Sparks dead. There was no doubt in his mind as to which one of them it was going to be. His blood quickened in his veins. His senses sharpened.

As he walked, his gait changed from the peddler's forthright stride to the lithe, stalking pace of a predator. He stood straighter, held the rifle in his hand with more authority. He swung the barrel up to rest on his shoulder and girded himself for what he knew would come.

He scratched at the uncomfortable, grit-catching beard, deciding it was time to do something about it, right after he finished with Sparks. He accepted the fact that he would not be permitted by Crockett and his boys to be a survivor, but, then, what other folks permitted had never made much of an impression on him. He had always cut his own trail, walked his own path.

Abruptly he turned down an alley and doubled back toward the saloon, stopping at the far corner. He waited a moment, aware that the heavy thud of footsteps had ceased among the dark shadows laced by pale light thrown from the saloon's upstairs windows. Then he heard a much lighter tread a few feet away. Someone farther back in the alley. His nerves tautened, senses prickling.

"I'm ready for you, Sparks," Kane stated flatly.

Dead silence. Ringing silence. Whoever else was in the alley was not about to show himself.

Kane figured Sparks to be just outside a pool of light less then ten feet before him. He figured wrong. It was a mistake. A mistake that could have cost him his life.

A dry chuckle, long and drawn out, rolled over Kane. There was no humor in that laugh, only the promise of death. At the same instant he felt a sharp jab in his side right beneath his elevated arm.

Tension rose between the two men who stood in the dark, each taking the other's measure. They were like a pair of stray dogs, each stiffly waiting, hackles raised.

"Glad you're here," the voice was low and quiet. "It would have galled me to have to chase you all over town."

He took the rifle from the peddler's hand, letting it down easy in the dust at their feet and pressed the knife more deeply into the man's side.

Kane didn't move. He felt the prick of the Bowie's tip and the answering warmth of his blood flowing onto its edge. Sparks lifted Kane's pistol from its holster, sending it to join the rifle. It didn't matter. Kane could deal with this kind of fight. One man pitted against another.

"You know better than that," Kane spit out. "I don't run from fights."

Sparks shifted his hold slightly, moving the knife around to rest against Kane's belly, gouging the point in just a little.

Kane, his eyes accustomed to the alley's dimness now, could see Sparks. The man's movement shifted him into a pool of light cast by one of the saloon windows. The outlaw regarded his old enemy from half-moon eyes. His face was deeply lined, like old leather, with deep furrows across the forehead and high cheekbones. The lizard eyes were dark and lifeless, hanging on Kane, and then, slowly, a smirk twisted his hard face.

"You sweatin' yet? You know what I'm gonna do? I got me a big knife here. I want you to feel the steel when it goes in. I want you alive long enough to feel it when I stick it in your gut and twist it up around your heart."

"I'm waiting."

"Don't expect me to believe you're that eager to die," Sparks said, and gave a nasty laugh. No play in his grip, no opportunity for Kane to turn the table. "Full of bluff then. Suits me. Think about it for a bit." He kept on smiling. "I heard a peddler come into town, an' he set to figgerin' on settlin' down." He shook his head. "Maybe you fell on hard times. Maybe I should pity you." He pulled a sympathetic face that was anything but, then flashed uneven teeth in a scavenger's grimace. "But I know better. What the hell you doin' in this boil on the backside of nowhere? Got your sights set on gunnin' somebody here?"

"I wasn't huntin' it in Cold Flats," Kane said flatly. "And I'm not looking for it now. But this is the end of the line. I'm settling in. I'm taking Crockett down to do it, and you're going to lead the way to hell."

Sparks bore heavily on the knife, but Kane had found his opening. He slid sideways, the knife ripping a groove in the flesh across his stomach as he swung a good, solid punch with his right hand and blocked the return of Sparks's knife with his left. It happened so fast Sparks grunted, first in surprise, then in pain as the peddler's fist connected.

That separated them, but did nothing to undercut Sparks' cock-sureness. "It's a good thing I'm gonna kill you. Crockett will thank me proper."

He waved the Bowie in front of his adversary like a threatening snake, the finely honed blade glinting wickedly when it caught the raw lamplight. The knife was a fourteen-inch monster compared to the eight inches of cold steel Kane drew from the inside of his boot with a smooth flourish as he slid into the shadows.

Kane was aware of the warm trickle of blood soaking his shirt-front. It was nothing, but he was going to have to be very careful. Sparks was a stupid man, letting vengeance pump his blood, but he was experienced and, with that Bowie in his fist, he would have the longer reach.

Sparks chuckled again as he caught a glint of Kane's steel. "What're you plannin' on doin' with that li'l toad sticker?" he goaded. Then he advanced, a big man with the heft behind him to slice that blade of his right through bone.

Kane fell silent, pacing himself. A knife fight could take time, and he was grateful for the privacy of the alley as well as the growing din that issued from the saloon.

Sparks moved in fast and a little clumsily, swinging the blooded blade in a wide arc. His opponent reacted with all the grace of a big cat and all the cunning of a wolf. He sucked in his gut and slid sideways again out of range, his own smaller knife coming into play only an instant to deflect the point of Sparks's larger blade.

Kane's enemy was a big man, pressing his weight to advantage, trying to force Kane into a corner from which he could not turn away. And, in the close confines of the dark alley, such a strategy just might work.

He jumped back before Sparks's lunge, leading him. Knife held low, he parried and retreated before a flurry of well-aimed thrusts and slashes, twisting and turning, conceding for the moment Sparks's superiority. He could wait for his own opportunity. In the mottled darkness their knives clinked softly together time and again. Kane's smaller knife slid against the larger Bowie in a vicious dance that set steel singing, the tone audible only to the two men locked in grim combat, the intensity of their concentration, one on the other, blocking out all other sound.

Sweat misted Kane's forehead, touched and cooled by the chill in the night air. His golden eyes locked Sparks's in their hypnotic gaze with a predator's promise of destruction as the bigger man came on, attempting to slash and cut his way through his guard. The long, thick blade of the Bowie wove a treacherous silver net; one that glinted with the promise of a lingering death.

Kane continued to back up before Sparks's onslaught, until, out of the corner of his eye, he spotted the outside wall of the saloon. From the beginning Sparks had pushed to get him into that corner, and he went with him.

Sparks's ability with knives was evident. But the wolf with the larger fangs and sharper claws did not always win the fight. There were times when it took guile and raw nerves, and Kane did not come up short on either one.

When things looked about right to him, the peddler stopped his retreat and stood his ground. Past knife fights faded into vague memories of children's games compared to what happened when he thwarted Sparks's attempts to drive him farther back into the corner.

"Think I'll just go ahead an' gut ya. Let you die real slow here in the dirt with your innards in your hands."

Kane smiled at the look of puzzlement Sparks was unable to conceal when the big man's knife flicked first here, then there, darting for a vital spot only to be deflected by the point of the smaller knife always there sooner. Speed and agility combined with an expertise that made the knife come alive in Kane's hands.

He nicked Sparks a couple of times, knife flicking out like a serpent's tongue to taste blood and cut deep enough to rattle the man's confidence as blood seeped up from torn flesh to soak his shirt. He sensed the fury in Sparks swiftly rising beyond control, and his lips parted in a wolf's grin as his old enemy drove in even harder on the attack. That was what he had been waiting for, what he had counted on. He side-stepped, spun, and dodged the sweep of the heavy blade, but he wasn't quite fast enough. The back slash caught him across the cheek, splashing blood onto his bristling beard in a scarlet spray first, then in a slow-dripping stream.

For a moment they broke. Both men were breathing heavily. Both were bleeding. Each man crouched and again took the other's measure.

Slowly Kane started to circle to the right as if to get clear of the corner, eyes glinting feral yellow in the pale lamplight. Sparks cut him off easily. With a leer he crowded his opponent, his knife making tiny circles in the air as he eyed his adversary much as a cat regards a mouse before ending the struggle. He had not finished the miserable peddler as easily as he had planned, and his confidence was not what it had been at the beginning, but his determination was no less dimmed.

Kane read his enemy and knew, if he played this out to the end, he would keep his hide whole. He changed tactics suddenly. Where he had been merely defensive since the fight started, now he was suddenly aggressive. The point of his knife leaped in again and again, reaching for Sparks's vitals. The smaller blade nipped dangerously close, slipping past the cold steel in Sparks's hand almost to its target.

For an instant Sparks was startled by the complete turnabout, dropping back a couple of paces before the sudden fury of Kane's attack. Kane took advantage of those painfully won inches, surging forward.

With a grunt Sparks abruptly stopped. Catching the peddler's smaller blade on the back of his Bowie, he held it there as they struggled, grunting, sweating, and bleeding, their faces only inches apart. Kane felt the hot, moist breath of his opponent on his cheek, felt the trip-hammer beat of his own heart and the warm ooze of his own blood. Allowing his blade to slip, he felt Sparks press forward, leaning into the new advantage. They toppled together into the dust, the tune of the saloon's tinkling piano filtering out into the alley. Locked together with his opponent in a death grip, Kane held every muscle rigid. He braced against the bigger man's weight like an ancient cone pine rooted in solid rock, resolute against the rising storm. Then, with no warning, he gave way, rolling backwards.

Sparks swore as he stumbled forward, tripped, and fell, unable to control his momentum.

His blade freed from the grip of Sparks's Bowie, Kane slammed into the ground and somersaulted back as Sparks slashed wildly at the air. There had been risks in this maneuver, and the battle-wizened man had known it. Consequently, Kane wasn't surprised when he felt the tear of his coat, his shirt, and the flesh underneath as he spun away from Sparks. They were cutting each other to ribbons. Blood, mingling with sweat, the feel of one not much different than the other now, followed the path of Sparks's knife along Kane's torn left arm. Sparks bellowed like a bull lucky enough to nick the bullfighter and lunged after his prey who was rolling to his feet.

Kane's strategy had included his being able to regain his feet before Sparks closed in on him again, but the man's speed was astonishing. He didn't give him the chance to climb back to his feet. He simply dropped on him, using his weight as a battering ram.

"Die you piss-ant of a peddler!"

The air burst out of Kane's lungs, and his smaller knife flew off into the dark shadows. His empty hand whipped up barely in time to snag Sparks's wrist in its descending arc. The outlaw's knife hand locked in his grip, Kane gasped, rallied, and shifted his weight beneath Sparks, using the bigger man's momentum to slam him into the saloon wall. In the instant that followed, he shifted his grip, completed the circle, and sank the Bowie into the outlaw's chest. Sparks gasped, eyes widening. There was one last wheezing sound before he died. It was fast, brutal, and it was final.

Seconds dragged past. Kane's own heavy breathing rasped in his ears as muscles rigidly strung in battle, relaxed to normal. He rolled to his hands and knees, head hanging, then climbed to his feet, the raucous good times in the saloon providing a backdrop to the thundering of his heart. He was bleeding freely, and every movement was an effort, though none of the wounds was serious. He bent over, swaying as he did so, and jerked the Bowie free from the chest of its previous owner. He was about to collect his guns and slip away into the darkness when something made him pause and look up.

"Sweet mother of mercy," he uttered the words in a groan, not sure if it had been a noise or some hidden inner instinct that had made him do it. But he looked toward the saloon's second floor from where the soft light issued and, there, staring down at him as if in a trance, was Samantha Cameron.

The instant she realized his eyes were upon her, she jerked back as if burned, slid the window quickly closed, and retreated out of the reach of Kane's burning, still battle-heated, gaze.

He glanced at the body in the alley, then back to the window. The Bowie gripped tightly in his good right hand, he holstered his pistol, shouldered his rifle, and started for the back stairs that led to her room.

CHAPTER
TEN

Descanso Cordova, more commonly known as El Diablo, sat at his table quietly nursing a bottle of whiskey. It had been a long, dangerous ride, coming up through Mexico, crossing the border to reach Saquarra, and he had arrived with every intention of getting himself thoroughly and enjoyably drunk. The desert town had little to offer by way of entertainment, but a resourceful man could always find something to interest him. A couple of raw card games were going on, an occasional painted lady walked by who might provide a distraction for the evening, and there was plenty of good whiskey.

Something to cut the dust from a man's throat had been the first thing on Cordova's mind when he hit town. Card games and women, he had decided, could wait for a while. There were few enough places where he felt he could allow himself the luxury of sloshing himself into a full-blown drunk without considerable risk to his life, so he planned on enjoying every minute of his protected existence in Saquarra.

He had retreated to a quiet corner where he could allow rot-gut whiskey free rein while unobtrusively watching the world go by through bloodshot eyes, when he had spotted the town peddler of newly infamous and growing reputation. Already well into his drinking, recognition had taken a few moments in coming. Nonetheless, there was no mistaking a warrior's set, his panther-like stride, and the lionized wolfish-gold of his eyes. The man obviously had his back up. A wicked smile curled Cordova's lips fixed on the rim of his glass. When Pike left, he followed him outside and was leaning against the wall of the saloon when the peddler left with a newly acquired tail in the form of a badman named Sparks. Through his whiskey haze he viewed Saquarra's previously isolated existence. Change was coming — it would take one form or another, but it was coming. The matter, he had decided right then, was going to require considerable thought and probably a hell of a lot more whiskey. He went back inside, bought a bottle this time, and he resumed his place at the table he had formerly occupied.

Attracted by his dark, good looks, one of the saloon's most heavily painted ladies sashayed up to his table while he lounged deep in thought. "I'm Vera, and you're a man who looks like he could use some company." She was small, still attractive, with coarse red hair and pale blue eyes. She moved close enough to envelope him with the cloud of her sweet-smelling perfume.

Cordova drew her onto his lap, encircling her with the arm not involved with the serious business of conveying his next drink to his lips. He felt the first stirrings of temptation in the tightness of his *vaquero's* pants. It had been a long time, and he was unaccustomed to such drought. But then there were priorities. He sighed.

"Ah, my flower, perhaps later . . . but for now, I am otherwise engaged."

Cordova urged her to her feet, regretting the loss of her willing warmth against him. He raised his full glass in a polite salute, because he liked women. He tossed it back and refilled it almost in the same motion.

Vera pouted and ran an enticing finger along his cheek as she bent very near, giving him a good view down the front of her dress. "You change your mind, honey, you just give me a wave."

She was gone from his thoughts almost the moment she floated away. Cordova, settling back, poured himself another drink, propped his feet up on the chair across from him, contemplating Frank Crockett who sat near the center of the saloon. His habit of watching people had given way to the matter concerning his own survival that had trained him never to forget a face. He prided himself on knowing every bandit, highwayman, and lawman between Mexico City and the Colorado River, and a few beyond. Some he knew well, a handful only by sight, and, while at times he rode with some and fought with others, he called none of them friend. He knew he was liked, his ribald humor appreciated around many camp fires. He vacillated between bandit and bounty hunter. The latter was one facet of his nature about which little was known, since none remained alive to talk about it. He enjoyed the twisted thought that there could very well be a bounty hunter on his trail even as he hunted another. He courted situations with the potential of a crate of old dynamite. When one came along, he would leap whichever way his impulse drew him, then played his cards out to the end. That was the life that made the blood sing in his veins. It was the danger that jacked him up, and he didn't much worry about right and wrong. His only truly defining characteristic was loyalty to a cause, once he championed it.

His gaze drifted around the inside of the saloon, his drinking not as advanced as he had planned upon his arrival. Lamplight shimmered off straight black hair as he tossed back another drink, watching Frank Crockett and Mississippi Pike, who had just strolled back in through the batwings. The look on Crockett's face was not one of approval.

"*Aie-yi-yi*," Cordova murmured to himself, only a little bit drunk. He saw his opportunity slipping away. Things were becoming too interesting to retreat into the haze of a drunken binge.

He knew both the big man and his *segundo* by sight from a previous visit to Saquarra. It had been evident at that time that Crockett was a man who clutched power to him, that the town was in his hip pocket, and, as far as he was concerned, nothing would alter that.

Cordova was observant. Even though he was drinking, the earlier exchange between the pair had not escaped his notice. In fact, it had been enlightening. Even more revealing was the fact that no one else in the saloon had seemed aware of a wolf on the prowl in their midst. And that was exactly what the peddler was in his mind. A *lobo*. In seconds Cordova had taken the man's

114

measure, given him a nickname — El Lobo — and felt his curiosity piqued. If that one caught Saquarra by surprise, who could say what would happen?

The situation was fascinating to Cordova, and he wondered idly if he should deal himself into the game. To be decided yet was with which side he should align himself. Neither El Lobo nor Crockett would back down, once they locked horns. El Lobo was but one man. Crockett had many more men. That stirred a sense of camaraderie and empathy with El Lobo in El Diablo's unpredictable heart. They stood on common ground. Both were loners; both were unpredictable. The devil and the wolf.

He rose, picking up his bottle and glass, sauntering in Crockett's direction. After all, there were those damnable priorities. Besides, he liked Saquarra just the way it was. It would be inconvenient to have it change. He stopped by the town boss' table.

"Mind if I join you, señor?" he asked, able to converse in perfect, unaccented English but allowing his words to slur slightly and the heavy Mexican accent of his home land to color his speech.

Frank Crockett, looking up from his cards, grudgingly acknowledged Cordova's presence. For a man aware of everything around him, it was an art — this turning a bland face to the world.

Observing the stranger approach Crockett, Mississippi had edged his way along the bar to within earshot.

"Something you wanted to say to me, mister?" Crockett put the question to Cordova bluntly, hardly giving him more than a glance before returning his attention to the cards spread on the table before him.

"Ah," Cordova said expansively, spreading his arms, the partially emptied whiskey bottle dangling from one hand. "I have much to tell you . . . and your fren'." He tipped his head in Mississippi's direction as Saquarra's *segundo* edged even closer to his boss' table. "He seems interested in what I say."

Crockett looked up from his cards again slowly and pinned Pike with his hard-eyed gaze, damning him for returning so soon after his earlier dismissal. "Mississippi, I'm tired of you reelin' around like a pup, trying to find a place to lie down," he snapped. "Now get your tail over here."

Pike started like he'd stepped on a raw egg, but swaggered toward the two.

"What the hell do *you* want, Mex?" Pike demanded before he even reached his boss' side.

The affable, alcohol-born grin froze in place on Cordova's face, and his voice found its edge. "Your fren'," he directed his remark to Crockett in an exaggerated sing-song, "does not seem friendly to El Diablo."

Cordova had been the butt of prejudice at the hands of *gringos* often enough to know he did not like it. Still, there were times when tolerance gained a man much. This could be one of them. There would be no refuge without Saquarra.

Exasperated, Crockett grunted and threw his cards down on the table. Both his solitude and his game had been interrupted, and there was no quick explanation forthcoming. His patience was rapidly wearing thin.

"Mississippi don't run things around here. I do. And it wasn't him you come over here to talk to. Now *I'm* listening. Suppose you tell me what the hell it is you want?"

Cordova's eyes narrowed, sparks jumping in their dark, soulless depths, but the ever-present grin remained fixed in place on the rigid, desert-etched contours of his face. He was reconsidering his earlier decision to let Crockett know what was brewing. But Cordova decided to allow events to progress in their own way.

"There ees a man in Saquarra who ees not what he seems," he finally said, setting down his bottle and glass with a thunk and a clink, pulling up a chair to straddle it, and crossing his arms over the back.

Crockett's exasperation did not lessen. "There aren't many men in Saquarra who want to climb up on a mountain and yell to the world who they are and where they're headed next."

Cordova shook his head. "The wolf walks among you," he said, and gave a full-throated, incredulous laugh. "And you, like a pack of dumb sheep, don't see him!" His crooked smile registered utter disbelief, and he rocked in his chair, before tossing down another drink.

Crockett found himself on the verge of violent anger as he faced the drunken, grinning idiot across the table from him. "Just who the hell is this man you're talking about?" he asked stonily, not sure he was even interested in the answer.

Quirking an eyebrow, Cordova almost giggled, and then tossed a nod in the direction of the saloon door. "You don't know, do you?" Another laugh, another drink. "He left here just a short time ago."

"Sparks?" Crockett demanded.

"No, the man who left before him. El Lobo."

A deep, measuring silence settled between the three of them, though the din of the saloon increased around them as more customers drifted in. Then suddenly Mississippi, pretty far into his own cups, exploded into laughter, his voice reverberating across the room. "He means that damn' tin-pan man," he snorted. Pike thought he would choke on the humor of it. The beer he drank threatened to come out his nose as he swallowed another hoot.

"El Lobo," Crockett sneered. "Mighty big handle for a damned no-' count peddler. He ain't worth a slop jar, far as I'm concerned."

Crockett didn't believe the hawker was anything more than he appeared to be. He certainly didn't appear to be a threat. The crazy bastard sitting across from him was another matter. He had a deadly reputation as a man who took incredible risks and lived, while his enemies did not.

Cordova chuckled, raised his bottle, and slopped more liquor into his glass. "No? You are not blind. You know he speaks to the good citizens of Saquarra."

"That tin-pan man ain't worth nothin'," Pike interjected boastfully. "Why, you should 'a' seen him

118

run with his tail tucked atween his legs when I slung a little lead over at the livery the other night. He was huddled in the horse manure like a rabbit."

Cordova threw his head back and howled. "Oh, *sí*, like a rabbit!" He laughed until he was breathless. "He was tricking you. He ees El Lobo, the wolf. I have named him." He smacked his lips after yet another drink. "And, gentlemen," he added with drink-sodden, mock sincerity, "he ees also crazy. But I think he ees crazy like a fox."

"You're drunk," Crockett said evenly, ending their exchange by returning his attention to the cards on the table.

"Want me to show him the door?" Pike asked with relish.

"He'll find it under his own steam. Looks bright enough."

"Oh, *sí*," El Diablo agreed, sobering despite the alcohol still pumping through his veins, his eyes narrowing. "El Diablo will find the door for himself."

Neatly avoiding Pike's grasp, Cordova came to his feet, wobbled, eyed the level of liquor in his bottle once again, then returned the stopper to its mouth. This was not the night for getting seriously drunk, after all, in spite of his having gone through a good part of the bottle. Besides, the pleasant buzz was wearing off. First, he would get some fresh air again, then perhaps some coffee. Then he would find El Lobo. The wolf and the devil would join forces. With some difficulty he straightened and made his way with dignity out into the street.

Pike followed El Diablo to the door, then resumed his place at the bar, still laughing over the claims the half-baked Mexican *bandido* had made. It was hard to believe men of his cut had razed Saquarra for so long before Crockett and his bunch had come along to change things. Pike had never met a Mex with any sand.

This time the cold night air hit Cordova like a slap in the face as he left the saloon. He drew it deeply into his lungs, clearing out a good part of the cobwebs almost instantly. The bottle was still cradled under one arm, but he was drinking no more. He would have to be stone-cold sober when he caught up with the one he had nicknamed El Lobo. He wanted to talk with him.

It was getting late, and the streets were deserted. Men who trod the boardwalks during the day now congregated in the saloon. The permanent residents of Saquarra were locked tightly inside their homes until daylight. Few of the townspeople patronized the saloon at any time other than in the middle of the afternoon.

Striding through the darkness, Cordova was wondering where he could get a cup of coffee so late in such a town when his footsteps carried him past the alley that ran alongside the saloon. There were pale spills of lamplight to illuminate its length just enough to highlight the shadows and draw a man's curiosity. There was something there, lying in the dust.

His senses sharpened, throwing off more of the dulling effects of the panther piss he'd been drinking.

"El Lobo?" he called softly, tension filling his body so that his hand instantly drifted to the gun at his hip.

120

He ducked down the alley, cat-footing it along within the shadows that hugged the sides of the buildings. He moved swiftly, senses alert, until the body was lying directly at his feet. It was Sparks. Cordova kept his back to the wall and moved very little, ears pricked to every small sound beneath the tinkling of the distant piano and throb of rough voices. He was at a disadvantage, his bottle cradled securely under one arm, his reflexes not at their best. Now was not the time to be caught unaware.

"You were a terrible fool," he murmured to the dead man at his feet.

Satisfied the alley was empty save for himself and the corpse, he bent over for a closer look. Sparks had been known as a knife man, and he had been killed with that weapon. The big Bowie the man usually carried in a sheath at his belt was nowhere in evidence.

Cordova stood erect and braced himself. So, the wolf had bared his fangs. He felt a surge of warmth course through him. He had to find El Lobo.

Turning to follow his thoughts, Cordova saw something glint in the dust of the alley near the saloon's back wall. He walked toward it, paused, and picked it up. It was a knife, a good, well-balanced knife — one good for many purposes, among them parrying the thrust of an oversize Bowie. El Lobo's knife had been lost, but the battle won. Hefting the weapon, Cordova slid it into his belt and headed for the peddler's wagon.

CHAPTER
ELEVEN

Samantha shivered, shuddered as she hugged herself, and stepped quickly away from the side window that overlooked the alley, nearly upsetting the small table nearby where the coal-oil lamp burned. She had seen men kill each other before, but a knife fight was a particularly vicious way to accomplish that end. What she had just witnessed she still found hard to believe. The peddler had killed a man. Maybe he wasn't a peddler. No simple peddler ever wielded a knife the way he had.

The chill that welled up inside her, when she glanced back toward the window, took her by surprise. She had seen him wrench the knife from the dead man's chest — and he had seen her. Their eyes had locked for long seconds, and she had not immediately associated that steely glare with herself. But that look had sent an icy arrow of fear through her heart.

She edged back to the window and peeked through the filmy, yellow curtains at the alley below. The body was still there, a darker lamplight-washed shape in the shadows. The huckster — or whatever the hell he really was — was gone. That fact, instead of being reassuring, sent another icy nip slithering up her spine an instant before she bolted to the door, sliding the latch securely home.

Then she backed away, slowly, one silent step at a time, eyes fixed on the chipped paint on the green door. What she had witnessed was so far removed from the dry humor and quiet manner of Kane that Samantha's thinking was all tied up in knots. It made her doubt her own judgment. And that angered her.

She straightened her spine and lifted her chin. "Well, peddler," she whispered, unable as yet to pin another label on him, "what are you going to do now?"

Ears straining to hear any movement outside her door, Samantha waited as the tinkling notes of the piano drifted up from below to provide an annoying distraction. In a town such as Saquarra this kind of act of violence didn't mean much, and ordinarily she wouldn't give it a second thought. But she had sensed something in Kane's face when he had seen her watching him. She remembered clearly his claim that he did not kill unless he was hungry, or unless someone or something was trying to kill him. *Liar,* she thought to herself. In Saquarra it was easy to assume self-defense. But her suspicions were aroused to tingling excitement, and she was having difficulty in ascribing that noble motive to Kane's actions. He simply was not behaving like a peddler.

Almost without realizing it, she began pacing the confines of her room, the music downstairs dimly resounding in her ears. She stopped abruptly. A footstep brushed the thread-bare carpeting outside her door. Instinctively she fell back across the tiny room, away from the scrape of sound, as if the added distance, small as it was, would protect her from what lurked in the hallway beyond the wooden door.

Her breath caught in her throat as she watched. The blade of a knife, still bloody, slid beneath the latch from outside and lifted it clear.

"Get away from my door," she snarled without thought. "I have a gun!"

She stood there empty-handed, shivering and bluffing, watching the door as fascinated as a mouse hypnotized by a snake.

A flick of the knife blade and a moment later her desert rescuer was inside the room, gently easing the door closed behind him. The huge, murderous knife was still clasped tightly in one hand, its point held low and tipped in her direction.

Samantha fought down a scream. Instead, she choked. He was covered with blood, something she had not been able to see looking down on the alley from her window. It was caked in his beard, crusting his arm, and still dripping from his fingertips in bright crimson splatters that hit the floorboards in a soft patter like the last heavy droplets of rain after a summer storm.

Her stomach folded in on itself. For long seconds nothing was said. Samantha stared while Kane held her in the grip of his steady gaze, golden eyes glowing with a feral light. Unmoving, Samantha waited, breathing fast, her pale blue eyes fixed almost trance-like on the knife's huge, stained blade. For the first time ever she began to wish that Mississippi was somewhere nearby.

That thought was almost as frightening as the knife clasped in Kane's hand.

Kane noted the room was neat but lacking ruffles or anything that could be called feminine. He regarded Samantha from behind a long silence of his own. She remained a stunning figure of a woman. But so stiff, so rigid, she appeared to have been carved from alabaster. Her finely boned face was cool and immobile. He could not read which of her emotions was dominant, fear or anger. The tilt of her head, the set of her firm jaw, spoke of anger, but her eyes, large and eloquent, telegraphed a very real fear.

His eyes took in the tiny room again in the pale glow of lamplight. He drew a deep breath. Although he did not trust her, he did not want her to fear him. It was a peculiar feeling, since in the past he had never objected to anyone fearing him.

"Are you planning on using that thing on me, too?" Samantha asked, managing to squeeze out the words in a reedy tone, her eyes never leaving the bloodied tip of the knife.

Ah, there it was, fear given form.

Kane lowered the knife and answered her question with a question of his own. "What're you planning to do about what you saw down there in the alley?"

Staring at him through wide, glassy eyes, Samantha hesitated, trying to gauge the response he expected from her. She failed to discern even a small hint in the stony, cold set of his face. Underneath, he was a hard man she decided, nothing like the affable hawker of household wares, the rôle he generally assumed.

"I haven't decided," she finally answered lamely. "I'm not exactly sure what did happen down in the alley." She chose her words carefully. "Maybe I should clean those cuts and bandage them before you permanently stain my floor. Then I'll decide."

Kane laughed, a low growl of sound. "Lady, you sure are somethin'."

She waved him into a chair and grabbed the pitcher and basin, splashing water into it as she took up a clean cloth from the washstand. She hovered a few moments, trying to decide what to do first. She began by cleaning the deep wound along his left arm. Using strips of linen from a stack in her wardrobe, she bandaged it tightly before looking more closely at the damage to his face and belly.

"I'll have to shave the beard to take care of that one."

Kane nodded. "It was getting annoying anyhow."

She picked up the straight razor Pike had left in her room. Once the blade was in her hand, Kane wondered if he should trust her to the task. Before he could object, she was shaving him with a deft swiftness that scraped jaw and chin clean of wiry whiskers in a more proficient manner than he could have done.

Samantha frowned at the result. He was a handsome man, or had been devilishly so, until her handiwork had revealed the wicked-looking slash that ran from temple to chin. "Needs stitches or you'll have an awful scar."

He agreed. "You done it before?"

She went to her sewing kit, returning with the necessities for the unwanted chore. She sighed, laying out needle, thread, scissors, and a bottle of whiskey.

"I've had my share of experience. I lived in Georgia during the war. I was thirteen when I stitched my first man. One of my brothers. He barely made it home with a saber wound in his side. Mama was sick. There was nobody else, so I did it."

"War tore a lot of families apart. At least you were there to help him."

"He died. Now sit still, or I'll crow-stitch off in the wrong direction."

She deftly threaded the needle, ran needle and thread through the alcohol, and bent to her task.

Kane grabbed the whiskey bottle and took a long pull. He noticed her hand trembled slightly as she carefully tilted his head back. He contemplated her face while she quietly worked, aware of the light floral scent which hung closely about her, wafting over him whenever she leaned near. It was very feminine and very pleasant. Then he suddenly remembered the Mexican he had seen outside the saloon.

"You see anybody else in that alley?"

"No."

He ground his teeth against Samantha's stitching of the torn flesh, at the same time unable to shake the notion that during the fight with Sparks he had been observed by another set of eyes besides Samantha's, that he had missed something of great importance down there in that alley.

"You know what's going on in Saquarra?"

She looked at him like he was the town dolt.

He gave her an exasperated look. "I'm not talking about the obvious."

"If you mean . . . ? I've heard you've been making a few friends . . . and a lot more enemies. Of course, considering what happened in the alley, I guess you could count one less enemy."

Kane grimaced as she neatly set her last stitch. "Things are gonna start happening here mighty quick. I think it might be better if what happened down there remains a mystery for a while."

Samantha hesitated, snipping the end of the thread. "One look at your face and it won't be a mystery for long. There. I'm done."

Kane pushed himself up from the chair and walked over to the mirror on the other side of the room. He studied his beardless reflection before agreeing with her. "I guess you're right."

Samantha remained silent and motioned him back to the chair, so that she could next work on the long knife weal across his belly. Luckily it had barely broken the skin. She cleaned the blood off, doused it with whiskey, and quickly wrapped a bandage around Kane's stomach. She was confused and, as usual these days, frightened. What was she going to do? Her window overlooked the alley. What would she say to Mississippi or even Crockett himself, if either asked if she had seen anything? Maybe it wasn't worth worrying about in a town like Saquarra. After all, would anyone even take notice?

"Lots of folks lost plenty during the war," Kane said, venturing to break her silence.

"My mother, father, and two brothers," Samantha replied grimly. "I have one brother left, but he's back in Virginia, trying to get a new start."

128

"I lost my mother, sister, and brother right after the war when things should have been quietin'," Kane offered. "They were killed by some die-hard raiders who took losing the war mighty hard and treed the town. It started me down the path I haven't gotten off since. Never really wanted to . . . until recently."

"Well, let me tell you, it's as much a mistake here as it ever was," Samantha spit out. "Now, you better get out of here before Mississippi decides to pay a visit."

She tossed blood-stained cloths aside and flipped the red water from the basin out the window, trying to avoid the body still below. She looked Kane squarely in the eye. "You could still start over somewhere else, you know. Saquarra has absolutely nothing to offer anyone. And from my experience most lawmen aren't too observant . . . if you think you have any reason to be concerned on that score."

Kane glanced up at her briefly before climbing to his feet, feeling considerably steadier. "You don't need to worry about that," he told her with wry amusement. "I've got the law on my side, always have. There are those who say I'm crazy, but I figure that kind of talk more often than not helps in situations. Your own Sheriff Brown knows what I'm about." He paused, watching her face, trying to figure out if what he was saying rather clumsily was reaching home. "If we can rally folks here, we'll take Saquarra back."

"If you can't, you'll end up dead."

"A risk I'm prepared to take."

Samantha bit her lip. Her curiosity was piqued. Every time she looked at him, he appeared less and less like a peddler. She knew the background of Saquarra, and it gave her a moment's pause to think of the foolhardiness of one man taking on Frank Crockett and his bunch.

She managed to get the words out at last. "Alone? You're going to rally this town alone?"

"I've got friends. I'm not really alone in this any more. That's why I need your silence. To protect the others. There are too many who might get hurt if we're caught flat-footed now. And about the man in the alley, Sparks? It was an old grudge and has nothing to do with Saquarra." Kane moved to the door and laid his hand on the knob. "You expecting Mississippi tonight?"

Samantha shrugged and replied: "I expect him every night." An uncomfortable feeling of shame washed over her as she said this to a virtual stranger standing before her. It was something she hadn't felt so acutely since the circumstances surrounding her life in Saquarra began. She felt the need to help this man get out of town before it was too late. Saquarra did something to you. It drained the life out of people, so that they were concerned only with surviving. Life got to be so it didn't have much meaning. Maybe she could save the peddler; he couldn't save her. She tried once again to set him straight.

"Most of the town wanted this arrangement, as far as I understand it. Guess it sounded simple when Frank Crockett approached the elders with the idea. All the people had to do was keep their mouths shut and pay out a small amount of money . . . small compared to the losses they had been suffering from the raids on the town. In exchange, they were to receive protection against the bandits and outlaws passing through. No problem, a gentleman's agreement. Half the town still swears it was the best thing to ever happen to Saquarra. Those people just aren't worth getting yourself killed over."

"Yeah, but the others are."

"Are they? My mama told me many times that, if I didn't look out for myself, no one else would. So I made my own way. I did just fine, too, until the stage I was on was held up, the driver killed, and I was brought here. Pike wanted me, paid for me, and there was no one to gainsay him. In the end, in this town, he was protection of a sort. The only way I could have been better off in Saquarra would have been to have Frank Crockett himself interested in me. But that doesn't mean I like it, and it doesn't mean I'm not looking for a way out. But even I don't want anybody to die for me."

"I didn't say I was doing this for you," Kane stated bluntly. Then he shrugged and continued: "Might be, if you wait a spell, Saquarra will turn out to be a pretty nice little town."

Samantha raised an eyebrow, feigning skepticism, though she was mostly hurt by his admission that he wasn't interested in helping her.

"You won't say anything?" Kane asked.

Samantha opened her mouth to reply when footsteps thudded in the hall.

"Mississippi," she gasped. "It's Mississippi."

Kane swore under his breath as Samantha slid past him to the door.

"He'll kill us both if he finds you here," she whispered in terror.

She stepped around him, grasped the knob, and turned it before he could reassure her that that wasn't in his plan. Then she was through the door and out into the hall.

"Hiya, honey," Mississippi's voice, thick with whiskey, issued from beyond the door. "Been waitin' for me?"

Samantha's response was so muffled Kane could not understand what she said.

"Let's go inside where we can have shome privacy," Mississippi slurred out.

"I think I'd like to have a drink first, Mississippi," Samantha's voice answered a little louder, a little more strident.

Kane did not wait to see what Pike was going to do. He turned to the side which was still open. His injured arm gave him a twinge, but he eased his body through the opening, hung from the sill a few moments, then dropped like a cat to the alley below. He landed on his feet, saw that Sparks's body was gone, and made his way among the shadows of the back alleys in the direction of the livery and his wagon. He knew he should be moving faster, but he could not help waiting for the explosion of activity he fully expected to issue from the saloon the moment Samantha opened her mouth to Pike. He had long before learned to count on the worst in people. Telling Pike what she knew was the only safe course for her to take. Rationally he accepted the fact that everybody tended to look out after his own hide first and the devil take the hindmost. It was human nature.

Footsteps thudded with a hollow ring on the boardwalk, running in front of the string of false-fronted shops lining the main street. Voices boomed out in laughter and shouts, echoing down the length of the street, joining with the din issuing from the saloon. A short distance away Mex-town was going strong as well. Saquarra was far from a sleepy little desert town come nightfall.

Kane reached the livery and started for the back corral where his wagon was kept when the sheriff stepped out of the livery's side door directly in his path. The peddler froze in his tracks, his hand instantly going to the hilt of the recently acquired Bowie, relaxing only a little when he realized it was Clive Brown facing him.

The sheriff gave him a good looking over, eyes appraising, settling first on one dried, rust-colored, blood-stained bandage, then another. "Looks like you tangled with a varmint," he said easily, but there was nothing easy about his stance.

Kane stared back at the sheriff, finding a new respect for the man. Injuries and Samantha Cameron notwithstanding, he could not afford to get caught at a loss. Had the sheriff been someone else with a gun pulled, he could have blown him away in a heartbeat.

"There was a dead body over behind the saloon that needed taking care of, Sheriff," Kane said in quiet response, his ears cocked expectantly for the sound of footfalls in the vicinity. "But it seems to have disappeared."

Clive chuckled. "I reckon it has."

Kane was taken aback, his expression suddenly guarded. "I don't follow you."

"Just saw Red Grissom. He said you'd had a bit of trouble, and he'd cleaned up after you."

"The gunsmith?"

"Yep. He puts some store in you, though I can't figger out why."

"There's Samantha Cameron to think about."

"Samantha won't say anything," the sheriff said with dead certainty. "She's walking a fine wire right now. Won't want to have a hand in starting any trouble."

"And how about you?"

Brown sucked in his cheeks and pursed his lips. "I been thinkin' about what you said before, and I'm about ready to stir things up."

Kane threw his arm around Clive's shoulders in a rare display of camaraderie. "Between us, Sheriff, we're gonna do a helluva lot more than that."

CHAPTER
TWELVE

Kane left Sheriff Brown, moving with a near-silent tread toward his peddler's wagon. They could wait no longer. Doing so would be more dangerous for himself and those who would align themselves with him. There were things he could use from the wagon, bits and pieces he would be needing with the coming of the new day. As he walked, he cataloged his inventory. Peddlers generally carried some guns for trade or sale, and he had his share along with a few knives, but those items weren't the focus of his thoughts. Amazing what his wagon carried in the way of weaponry. There was some coal oil, gunpowder in a couple of small kegs, needles and lady's hairpins, nails, alcohol, a couple of latigos, and a pair of spurs. There was more. Much of it usable, if a man put his mind to it.

Deeply ingrained instinct caused him to approach the wagon with caution, although he wasn't expecting to find anything amiss. However, the night had been a busy one, and there was no telling what he might have stirred up along the way. A flutter of alarm suddenly sprang to life in him as he neared the wagon, and tiny hairs stood up keenly along the back of his neck. The familiar roll and prickle. He slowed his stride instantly and shifted the direction of his approach to the only partially blind side it had, the driver's box.

There remained a pale splash of moonlight to guide him, but the shining orb would not be up much longer, and with moonset the night would become fathomless. Whatever the problem, Kane intended to take care of it fast.

He edged along the building, uneasiness growing, tension settling in his shoulders and curling his fingers inward toward the gun at his hip. Suddenly a voice scraped across the night, freezing him in his tracks.

"Pssst! *¡Señor!* Wait!" No threat in that voice, and it was distinctly feminine. "I must speak with you."

A darker shape separated itself from the blackness between the buildings, moving swiftly toward Kane who moved to intercept her, drawing them both back into the deeper shadows. He immediately recognized the face turned up in the pale moonlight. It was Aniceta Esquivel, the mother of the boy he had dragged from beneath the hoofs of the outlaws' horses.

Nerves stretched taut, Kane tempered his tone which threatened to be sharp, laying his hands gently on her shoulders. "What is it?"

Although slight of stature she stood firmly beneath his touch. No female reticence or coy trembling here.

"I was hurrying home after I delivered some sewing *Señora* Jenks wanted *pronto*. I saw you in the alley . . . as you left *Señor* Sparks."

Kane grimaced. "I'm sorry."

"No! No! That is not why I stopped you here! I saw more." She dropped her voice even lower, the whisper

136

barely audible to his ears. "A man came to the alley after you went into the hotel. He looked at *Señor* Sparks and picked something up from the dirt. Then he left."

"You saw who it was?" He looked around quickly as he spoke to the woman. He could not shake the feeling other eyes were watching them now.

"*¡Sí, sí!* I followed him."

"That could have been a very dangerous thing to do."

She waved away his protest. "You are a good man. There are others on both sides of the deadline who would do the same. The man I saw is one of that Crockett's guests. He went to your wagon. I stayed here to watch. He is still there. I felt I must warn you."

Kane's eyes slid in the direction she indicated, narrowing, the gold in their depths reflecting the waning moonlight. "*Gracias.* You better go now. I'm sure your son's waiting for you, and it is dangerous for you here."

She nodded, then placed a small, strong hand on his arm. "Be very careful, *señor*."

Kane smiled. "I always am."

He waited until she was out of view before he turned. There was something in the air, a disquiet that assured him that the outlaw was still just where she said he was. Barely a heartbeat passed between that certainty and the sight of a knife blade flashing in the faint light spilled by the moon. It arched out of his wagon, landing with a solid thunk next to Kane on the hard-packed earth. He knew what it was even before he could see it clearly. It was the knife he'd lost in the alley during the fight with Sparks.

"Hey, El Lobo!" a voice called softly from the wagon. Low and almost sing-song, it did not carry far. "El Lobo, are you listening? I wish to talk." The Mexican accent, though subdued, was unmistakable.

A whiskey bottle with a white cloth tied loosely about its neck was thrust out of the back of the wagon and waved slowly back and forth, the glint of the glass and flash of the white cloth stark against the backdrop of the night. "I want to parley."

No more than ten feet from the wagon Kane was positioned farther out in the open than he cared to be, darkness his only real concealment. He wondered what the hell that fella was talking about. El Lobo? He had been called a lot of things in his time, but never had that been one of them.

"What do we have to parley about?" He paused a moment, feeling the quiet. When he spoke again, it was with unquestionable authority. "Put down that bottle, throw out your gun, and come into the open. Then we'll talk."

"You are a hard man, *señor*."

Cordova gave his bottle a quick wave, the white cloth fluttering from its neck before he put it down and climbed out of the wagon, considerably sobered from his earlier state. He held his hands wide from his body, not eager to draw the fire of this man by accident. The old burning sang in Cordova's blood as it surged, cleansing itself of the last lingering effects of the alcohol, and he smiled. "You truly are a wolf among

138

the sheep. And they are so convinced of their own savageness that they are not even aware of you, are they, El Lobo?"

Kane's hand rested on the butt of his gun as he regarded the man before him, nerves stretched bow-gut tight. He didn't know what he was facing here. That the fellow in front of him had just leaked in out of the landscape could not be denied. He was one of Crockett's guests, dark-complexioned, face deeply lined, and eyes a funny brown that glinted wickedly even in the odd, mottled light. The man was obviously entertaining some thoughts of his own.

"Now that you've told me who I am, suppose you tell me who you are?"

"Many call me El Diablo." Cordova's eyes gleamed like chips of broken glass. His face folded and smoothed in the deep shadows with the changing play of expression. Amazingly straight, white teeth flashed with a smile that harbored no humor. "You are what everybody in this town ees talking about," he observed genially.

"I know what I am," Kane repeated. "I want to know what it is that you want."

"I want nothing."

"Then why are we here?"

Kane felt a little off balance and had no doubt that was exactly what the other man wanted him to feel.

"I was sitting in the saloon, getting quite pleasantly drunk, when I saw you. I decided, after some thought, that the devil and the wolf should drink together. You're going to need help."

"I've got some help."

"Not like the kind I offer, *señor*."

"Why do you want to help?"

"Let us just say it ees because little Aniceta ees so loyal to you." He broke eye contact with Kane for a moment, searching the dark clefts and crevices for watchful eyes. "And I am not pleased with *Señor* Crockett."

What did this El Diablo mean by that, Kane wondered. Saquarra sure was full of puzzles. First Samantha, then the sheriff, now this man. He eyed the area around him, all of his instincts fully aroused.

"You want me to trust you because you admire Aniceta and you aren't pleased with Crockett?"

Cordova laughed softly, still taking pains to keep his hands wide from his body. "You are here. I am here. The town ees here. Trust your instincts . . . you are the wolf."

It was a funny thing. When Kane met El Diablo's eyes, he trusted him. At least for this time, in this place. He nearly shuddered with the power of the force that suddenly connected them. They were not brothers, but they were nevertheless bound.

Cordova patted the gun low-slung at his hip, and grinned. "It ees likely the best offer you'll get in Saquarra."

That was a gold-plated fact. Many in Saquarra sided with him. A few were even willing to back that up with old guns, or anything else they could lay their hands on, but none would come packing El Diablo's outlaw background and abilities. There would be no telling

140

how the good folks of Saquarra would jump when the lead started flying. He felt that with El Diablo he would at least know that much. And all of a sudden that made all the difference in the world to him. It had been a long time since he had cared or even thought about whether he lived or died. But now he cared. This town was worth fighting for. This was where he was going to stay.

Kane gave a curt nod, his gut feeling solid with his decision. "All right. There's a lot to do before morning."

"That soon?"

"Too many eyes watching," Kane acknowledged. "Too many good people at risk if I let them in at the start."

"*Sí*, that ees so."

With the flowing, even stride of his newly acquired namesake — El Lobo — Kane started again for his wagon. Cordova allowed his hands to drop and fell in step beside him.

"You know we're as apt to get ourselves killed as we are to succeed," Kane remarked as he lowered the tailgate of the wagon and jumped lightly up inside. He settled a battered, dusty brown Stetson on his head and, as an afterthought, dragged out an odd-looking scatter-gun, tossing it to El Diablo as he jumped down.

"No doubt of that, my fren'," Cordova chuckled, snagging the weapon out of the air. "But such a thing has been true in the past, and El Diablo ees still here." He hefted the unique gun, then held it up in a gesture of thanks. "*Gracias.*"

"*De nada*," El Lobo returned.

CHAPTER
THIRTEEN

Dawn spilled out across the desert like an overturned jar of honey. The warm, golden light showed itself across the land and around the hilltops long before the sun was visible, heralding the blazing heat of the new day.

"Ah! Do you feel it, El Lobo? We are truly alive when we face death!"

Kane grunted, wondering (not for the first time) about this crazy, exuberant Mexican he had acquired by his side.

They walked together in the changing light, heavily armed, shoulder to shoulder. The devil and the wolf. Before the sun was fully risen in the eastern sky, they would either have Saquarra turned on its ear, or they would both be dead. The two of them were wound as tightly as new watch springs. They had slept little, sharing the close confines of Kane's wagon like old friends. Now their footsteps fell in even rhythm, and puffs of dust rose from beneath the soles of their boots.

Kane glanced at El Diablo. They were, Kane believed, cut from the same cloth. The outlaw's battles had not been the same ones that he had fought, but there was little difference in the fight for survival. El

142

Diablo had the same depth of experience buried within him. He was a man with that extra edge. Every gunslick that lived very long did. Without it, the odds were stacked against him before he began. Of necessity, the talent was forced to take a different form in each man, but Kane sensed it in the outlaw as he walked beside him, their strides matched, toward the saloon. The very air was electrified, crackling with power just as it did before an intense storm. One man sparked the other, and they continued on.

El Diablo hitched a breath in response to the tautness he felt in his chest, but the mood was about to break, and, when it did, he would move like a panther, all sinew and lusty invincibility. He was more centered in himself than El Lobo, and he knew that. He did not reach ahead. Did not plan beyond the obvious. He would confront what came when it did, and his response would be explosive. They were going to take the kinks out of this old town, and he was going to enjoy doing it. It somewhat surprised him how strongly he was coming to feel about that. He caressed the strange, revolving, sawed-off shotgun which El Lobo had dug from beneath the wagon's floorboards. It felt cool in his hands, and, providing four shots instead of two, it was a formidable weight he carried. El Diablo grinned.

The two men strode forth, Kane with easy assurance, Cordova with barely contained restless energy, both intent upon what was to come. There was no doubt in either that they would take Crockett down, for doubt bred failure, and failure meant death.

A curious face appeared in the general store window as they passed. A couple of early risers spotted them and drifted along, following at a distance. One slipped off from the others, cutting down an alley between buildings. Wherever that one was going, it wouldn't matter. It would be all over in minutes.

In the pale golden light of the coming day, Sheriff Brown stepped off the short boardwalk in front of his office, falling into step with El Lobo and El Diablo. He wore a gun at his hip and toted a Winchester rifle. As he came up alongside, he dug in his vest pocket and withdrew a couple of tin stars.

"You boys are gonna need these," he remarked, flipping one to each of them.

Wordlessly, Kane pinned his on his jacket.

El Diablo stuck his to the underside of his lapel, allowing the coarse brown fabric to flop back into place as they continued on.

"He's still there?" Kane posed the question to the sheriff.

"Yep."

El Diablo swung the shotgun up. "We could just kill him and end it."

"Nope."

Now Kane grinned, a tight grimace. "Sheriff's right. If we're gonna bring back law to this town, we have to do it right." He gave El Diablo a half apologetic, cock-eyed grin and a little latitude. "We kill him only if we have to."

"Might have to," was El Diablo's retort.

144

"Not likely," Sheriff Brown countered, gracing El Diablo with a sweeping appraisal. Then he directed his next remark to Kane. "You sure we can depend on this one?"

"You wound me!" El Diablo shot back at Sheriff Brown before Kane could respond.

"I don't *know* you."

"He'll stick," Kane interjected as they continued their walk, the saloon looming now before them. "But he might just kill Crockett."

The sheriff swore softly.

They paused a moment before the door. A couple of hard-looking men wandered out, no doubt heading for their bedrolls. Neither paid any attention to the knot of three men as they passed. Townsfolk were no longer visible, wisely now keeping to cover.

Kane checked his Winchester repeater, a match to the one the sheriff was carrying, and allowed his hand to brush the butt of his Colt tied down on his right thigh.

He glanced at El Diablo. The man's eyes glittered with anticipation. His hand showed white in its grip on the scatter-gun.

"You know, *señor*," El Diablo said amiably, "I approached Crockett before I saw you."

"Figured as much," Kane returned. "Why'd you choose me?"

Why? It was a complicated question with only seconds for El Diablo to consider it. There was no simple answer. A lifetime of vacillating between the fine hairs of the law had brought him to this point. Years of tasting the danger that brought a man closer to death because, to El Diablo, that was the only way for a man truly to taste life. If he never came close to death, never felt the blood pounding in his veins, or his lungs tearing raggedly with each rasping breath, then he was not fully alive. That was how he had become El Diablo. He could not live without the risks, the raw, nerve-fraying fights he threw himself into, one after another. He reveled in walking away intact from something no one had a right to walk away from at all. Because of that, once he settled in, chose a side, no matter how tight it got, he stayed through to the finish. In fact, the worse it got, the better it felt. The exhilaration was like flying free, then crashing abruptly to earth at its end, and beginning all over again. Then, of course, there was Crockett to be considered. He had never had much to do with him, and his encounter on the previous night had convinced him of his contempt for the man.

"I like you better," was his response to Kane's question.

"I need a drink," the sheriff said sourly, shaking his head at El Diablo's flat statement.

"Maybe you can get one before the shooting starts," the gunman suggested.

"Let's go," said Kane, taking the lead, straight-arming his way through the batwings into the saloon's quiet, dim interior.

Sheriff Brown was right behind him, a large, blocky contrast to the peddler's lean build and fluid stride. El Diablo appeared more independent in his actions, his presence more obvious than his build. His long, straight black hair flowed back over his shoulders in a mane. Having entered behind them, El Diablo immediately put a wall to his back, surveyed the scene with glittering eyes, then strode over to the bar.

The sheriff hesitated, scrutinizing the room, then moved off as Kane continued on without breaking stride. Golden eyes taking in all there was to see, Kane spotted Frank Crockett standing over by the bar, the table he had occupied earlier deserted, but the cards still spread out as if the big man had just gotten to his feet. Scattered around the room were a few men Kane did not recognize, and several were Crockett's men. Most of the latter were watching the peddler uncertainly, and they were slow on reaction time.

Kane altered his steps slightly and kept on walking.

"Hey," one of the gunmen said to his companion as he straightened from the bar, "that pilgrim's armed like he's goin' to war."

"Sheriff's here. Ain't gonna be no trouble," his friend reasoned.

Another of Crockett's cold-eyed men sat in a corner, feet propped up on a table, a nearly empty beer glass in his hand, while another, half way down the stairs leading to the saloon's second floor, stopped, watching the peddler.

Five men, plainly not attached to Crockett, were just drawing a card game to a close with the clink of silver and low grunts of exhaustion when Kane's gaze swept over and past them, touching momentarily on Red Grissom, giving the bartender a hard time.

That slowed Kane as he watched the exchange, marveling at Grissom who did most anything he pleased despite the town's occupation by Crockett and his boys. He wondered why it was that Grissom was still alive.

Out of the corner of his eye, time condensing into something not at all resembling its normal flow, Kane spotted Samantha. She was standing at the head of the stairs on the landing overlooking the saloon below. She wore a full burgundy velvet dressing gown, primly high at the neck. Mississippi stood next to her, his back to the room below unaware of the recent arrivals in the saloon below. Kane had been aware of Samantha's eyes on him from the moment he had set foot within her field of vision.

Samantha gaped when she spotted Kane coming through the door with the sheriff and that damnable Cordova. Whatever he had been before he'd been a peddler, it sure as hell hadn't been a peaceable profession. He was armed for war and walking confidently over to Crockett who did not even bother to turn his head at the sound of approaching footsteps. Whatever was about to happen down there would not be good. Her throat went dry, and her body stiffened.

That was enough to tip off Pike. "What the hell you lookin' at?" he growled at her.

Samantha could feel her knees quake as Mississippi turned his attention to the barroom below. She wanted to believe herself braver than this. The war and all her travels thereafter had combined to make her stronger. At least that was what she had always told herself. How else could she have gotten the courage to go on? But now, the peddler had pierced her armor, and somehow the sand was running out. She felt fear she had not experienced since the South had surrendered, and it left her shaken.

Kane's stride had been slowed, not stopped, and he advanced steadily on Crockett, wishing his attention was not divided. The potential was there for innocent people to get hurt, and he would not like to see it happen to Samantha. But whatever the outcome, he and Brown and El Diablo were moving, and there was no turning back.

Another two steps and Crockett turned from the bar into the barrel of Kane's Winchester. It pressed coldly against his belly. His amber eyes slid over Kane, then past him, fixing a moment on El Diablo, then on the sheriff. Nothing in his bony, angular face betrayed any emotion.

"You want something, tin-pan man?" he asked pointedly, and his hand rested near the butt of his gun.

Kane smiled a twisted smile. "You're under arrest."

Crockett shrugged and glanced at Kane, pinning him as a man who's just lost all his senses. Then he looked at El Diablo who stood with shotgun at the ready, lounging near the door. Finally his eyes came to rest on Sheriff Brown, braced now beneath the stairway, weaponry ready.

"You're dead men," Crockett said at last, a low grumbling groan of speech. "All three of you are dead men."

Kane thinned his lips and lifted a shoulder. "Maybe," he agreed, "but it's your belly my rifle's pointing at, and, if you don't get moving, you'll be just as dead."

"The town's full of my men. The saloon is full of my men. How far do you think you'll get?"

"Over to the jail," Kane said, a definite grimness in his tone that had been absent until now.

Crockett's men were shifting their positions nervously, awaiting some kind of signal from the big man.

Kane dug the barrel of his rifle in a little deeper. "You want to try your luck? Give 'em a nod, and I'll pull this trigger just like reflex. You won't live to see if they get me or not."

Crockett ignored his words, his eyes fixed now on the Mexican at the end of the bar. He was the one who had warned him of this. "I'll give you five hundred dollars if you pull that trigger," Crockett directed at El Diablo.

El Diablo sighed, his attention divided, his blood surging, though he preserved an outward calm. "You wound me, señor. I am not much, but I am loyal. And there ees this to consider." He flipped his lapel over, revealing the silver glint of his badge. "I have great respect for the law. Besides, even if I pulled the trigger on my friend, El Lobo, he would still blow a hole in your belly the size of my fist. And then," he smiled sadly, "I would not get paid."

"What about you, Brown? You don't really want to try to hold this town together again, do you? You can spill this peddler's blood, or you can watch it flow in the streets, spilling from the innocents you're so

150

worried about. And for what? They aren't lawmen like you."

Clive's jaw tensed, his hazel eyes flat and hard. "You've seen their badges. They're legal."

The tension in the saloon was thick. The scattering of Crockett's men was cocked and ready, but waiting for a signal from their boss. None was likely to chance not getting paid, and Kane silently thanked El Diablo for that wry remark.

"You're all crazy," Crockett said irritably, eyes flicking over the saloon, evaluating the situation. It wasn't good. But it was his town, dammit! Anger boiled up within him at the impasse he faced. He hated being forced to bend to another's will. Under the circumstances there was nothing else to be done. Nothing that wouldn't cost him his life. There would come another chance. He would have to wait them out. He was about to tell his men just that, but it was too late.

A lean, bristly, brown-haired man on the stairs, feeling himself in the clear for an instant, saw his chance to usurp and replace Mississippi as Crockett's right hand. He went for his gun.

Guns emerged from every corner of the room. But it was an explosion of more than guns as the suspense in the saloon burst like an over-ripe blister, sending the stand-off into chaos. El Diablo's shotgun kicked in his grasp. The brown-haired man on the stairs jerked, then took a headlong dive over the banister, the roar of his weapon background for the explosions of other guns. Dragging a heavy table over and rolling it in front of him, Kane's newest ally went to one knee behind it as a bullet splintered the bar beside him. The sheriff threw his blocky bulk prone as a bullet stitched a path where he had been standing, then he rolled with incredible agility to the cover an overturned table could provide.

"Get down!" Kane bellowed in the same instant in Samantha's direction where she was already moving, diving for the floor, small blotches of her burgundy dressing gown the only thing visible through the banister overhead.

Red Grissom vaulted over the bar, settling down behind it near the bartender. Kane floored Crockett with a brutal shove of his rifle barrel and followed him down, landing on top of him with enough power to force the air from the other man's lungs and leave him gasping as a bullet whistled past his ear.

Scrambling to his knees, the peddler shifted his rifle, drawing his attention in Mississippi's direction. He would have dropped Pike right then and ended it, if he had had a clear shot, but Crockett's *segundo* had hit the floor right along with Samantha and was now elbowing his way quickly along the landing, heading for the stairs. Kane threw a couple of shots in Pike's direction to make him nervous, as El Diablo's shotgun roared again, its sound like a cannon in the close confines of the saloon. Clive's Winchester cracked loudly, drawing a swarm of pistol shots in reply.

Kane knew they had to settle this fast and get Crockett over to the jail before the rest of the town's visiting outlaws realized what was going on and joined Crockett's forces. If that happened, the odds of the

152

three of them coming out of it alive would get mighty slim. It wasn't the dying that stuck in his craw; it was not finishing what he started out to do that didn't set well.

Crockett, breath returning, was beginning to stir, and Kane grabbed one of his arms, wrenching it tightly behind the town boss's back. In almost the same movement he twisted around, throwing a shot from his rifle like he would have from a six-gun. A sharp yelp and a growling curse followed, and the yahoo trying to slink up on him from behind was looking for new cover. Another bullet slammed into the bar above his head, peeling off splinters the size of kindling.

More guns exploded, eliciting screams from a couple of the saloon girls who had taken refuge behind the bar along with Grissom and the bartender. Another volley. A pale young woman in an emerald green fancy dress, cut low in front and short at the hem, jumped up from behind the bar, hands clasped over her ears, bolting for the door as another round of gunfire erupted. She ran right into it, dropping soddenly to lay unmoving in a spreading puddle of blood.

On the stairway Mississippi let loose and rolled down the risers as El Diablo spotted him and again discharged the shotgun with a reverberating roar. Below, on the saloon floor, Kane looked up and saw it was not a direct hit, but Pike had to have been stung. He knew well the pattern of that particular shotgun, and El Diablo could not have missed completely at that range.

Concern for Samantha flashed through his mind, but for the moment there was not a thing he could do for her save hope she hadn't been caught in the scatter-gun's spread. At least Pike, curled into an almost impossible spot behind the piano at the foot of the stairs, was down on the main floor, drawing the line of fire well away from her.

El Diablo pulled back, his hand drawing the gun at his hip, deciding to save the final round in Kane's scatter-gun. Six-gun in one hand, scatter-gun clutched in the other, he crabbed, scuttled, and bulled his way across the open spaces to where Vera, the saloon girl who had promised much, had fallen. Bullets continued to sing and thud all around him, leaving him miraculously untouched. He was breathing deeply, regularly, when he reached her, blood racing in his veins, aware of the hurried throb of his own heart and the pulsing in his ears because of it. It was the battlefield rush he craved, and he knew in that moment he had chosen the right side. It only gave him slight pause when he recognized the girl, realized she was dead, and he rolled immediately for new cover behind a table near the back door. El Diablo wanted to howl with barbarous fervor, give in to the killing fever that fired his blood, but he stifled it as El Lobo heaved himself and Crockett, arm still pinned behind his back, to their feet, muzzle of his rifle rammed beneath the big man's chin.

"One more from anyone and I'll blow his head off!"

The room fell deadly silent in the space of an instant. The clock, as Kane cocked his gun, was sharp and audible. Into the silence Crockett spoke.

154

"Back off! This crazy bastard'll do it. You can do something about this later, so just back off!"

Crockett's breath caught for an instant, then found its way around the cold steel barrel jabbing into his throat. His stomach clenched, and sweat rose instantly in a veil over him, but his face remained as impassive as stone. He knew everything could end right here in an eyeblink, but, if it didn't, the face he put on now was the face that would be remembered. It would determine his future in Saquarra.

Mississippi, crouched behind the piano, gun poised in his fist, wouldn't have hesitated to be the cause of Crockett's death. In fact, it would have pleased him greatly, but he had to consider and plan. He had to display the loyalty of a lieutenant if he hoped soon to become a general. More importantly, with Crockett on the fence, the reins of command would pass to him. The men would get used to taking orders from him, and from there it would only be one more step to make the arrangement permanent.

"All right," Mississippi called authoritatively from his place of concealment, "you all heard Mister Crockett. Hold your fire, boys, an' let 'em pass."

Kane kicked the overturned table nearest him out of the way and started backing Crockett toward the batwings.

Red Grissom appeared above the bar, face flushed a deep red, flashing evidence of the reason for his nickname. "You better go out the back," the gunsmith advised.

"Excellent idea," El Diablo agreed.

The sheriff eased from behind his table at the end of the bar, backing toward Kane, rifle at the ready. Brown's outlaw deputy kept the scatter-gun leveled at the room and watched carefully as his companions worked their way toward him. He thought about the jail as they edged toward him, Kane dragging Crockett by his bent arm, the sheriff swinging his Winchester to keep the room in his sights.

The sheriff was in the lead going out the door, looking first one way, then the other, to see that it was clear. Kane and his prisoner followed. Finally, El Diablo backed out the door, slamming it forcefully at his exit as he turned to catch up with the others.

The whole time El Diablo was still thinking about the jail. It was the only place in town where they could secure Crockett, but it could also be a death trap. El Diablo had frequently plunged into battle with what appeared to be a crazy recklessness, but he would not be cornered. The idea sent a chill up his spine. He would see, and he would decide. But whatever he decided, he would not risk what a closed in space could do to him. He would permit no one to see the devil's weakness.

CHAPTER
FOURTEEN

The group led by the sheriff hadn't gone fifty yards when they became aware of a small gathering of onlookers clustering in their wake. Some just stood and stared, eyes hungrily following their progress toward the jail. Others tagged along, a certain wariness dragging at their footsteps. Kane recognized a few of the faces: some of Saquarra's better citizens, at least ones in possession of a conscience. They were opposed to Frank Crockett's rule.

A galvanized force seemed to be running through the town as the crowd gathered in numbers, and a few members of the Mexican community ventured across the deadline in the wake of the bloody confrontation in the saloon.

The trio continued their walk to the jail, a defiant Frank Crockett held before them, striding forth with a steady, confident gait. The crowd gained in numbers until it was joined by a contingent from Mex-town. Then began the rumbling of discontent among some of the Anglos who started dispersing to the sides. Other townsfolk fell back as they approached the jail, averting their eyes from Crockett whose hard stare was making it very clear he would remember these faces of betrayal.

"There are the good people of Saquarra," El Diablo said, his words dripping with contempt. "We will give their town back to them, and they will shun us."

Crockett laughed. "You know them well."

"Yes, but I know you better, señor, and I prefer to be shunned by them."

"They're a little afraid of you, Mex, because you're fast with a gun, but they don't like you, and you'll never have their respect. You're just another greaser with a gun."

Kane fully expected El Diablo to pull the trigger and silence Crockett permanently. But it didn't happen. They walked up the wooden steps to the jail, the ring of their boots decisive in the heavy silence that followed Crockett's remark. Clive opened the door ahead of them. Then they were all safely inside.

In the eerie aftermath of the saloon fight Samantha climbed unsteadily to her feet near the head of the stairs. She was dumbstruck at the carnage, the sounds of the guns still echoing in her ears. The saloon floor resembled a battlefield. One of Frank Crockett's men was sprawled grotesquely in a pool of his own congealing blood at the base of the stairs where he had fallen. One of the poker players, who had occupied the far corner nearly all night long, was dead as well. Vera, who had run the upstairs business, was silent now, too. Samantha had despised her, but she had not deserved this.

Gripping the banister, Samantha stared down into the room, for the moment too mesmerized to notice the blood on the sleeve of her own dressing gown, or to pay attention to the sting where a couple of stray pellets had caught her. When she did, it seemed inconsequential.

From nearby a low moan clawed at her ears. *Jesus,* Samantha thought to herself, *what has that peddler brought about in Saquarra? First there was the knife fight in the alley, now this. What kind of man is Zachariah Kane?*

The survivors were moving slowly below, muttering curses and shoving furniture aside. Another of Crockett's nameless men arrived to investigate all the gunfire. He met with Mississippi and two of the card players. Samantha was out of earshot, but a rapid exchange passed among them. With the exception of Mississippi, Crockett's men left the saloon.

Near the back door the bartender, Harlan Moody, and Red Grissom were huddled in a furious exchange. Samantha would have edged closer to hear what they were saying if Mississippi had not turned just then and started in her direction, a set, angry look contorting his features.

He climbed the stairs, passing the blood splatters caused by El Diablo's scatter-gun when the first of Crockett's men was taken down. Flecks of red on Mississippi's sand-colored shirt along his left arm and shoulder held Samantha's gaze as he advanced toward her, the eerie creak of the stairs accompanying his steps. All else was silence. Samantha could see his growing anger. She could try to run, but it would do no good, so she remained frozen in position, engulfed by a feeling of defeat.

"Are you all right?" Samantha managed to ask cautiously. Her words clunked like pig iron tossed in a smith's kettle.

Mississippi fastened his hands onto her shoulders and brutally jerked her. "Bitch!" He hissed the word, glaring and shaking her roughly. "You knew what he was planning. You knew from the beginning."

"No," Samantha protested.

Mississippi cut her off. "Don't lie to me!" He roared a barrage of curses, accenting each word by pushing the tips of his fingers into Samantha's collarbone, forcing her to back up with each painful jab.

Samantha attempted to move out of range, but she could not outpace him, and he continued at her, fingers gouging into her tender flesh.

Pike slapped her with ringing force. "Don't lie to me!"

Her skin burned from the slap, and her heart pounded out her terror.

"Why don't you leave her alone, Mississippi?" Red Grissom's voice carried strongly from below.

"Shut up, Grissom," Pike snarled back. "You think I need an excuse to put a bullet in your head?"

Turning, Mississippi stalked off down the hall toward Samantha's room, her wrists clenched in his fist. She fought the painful grasp in which he held her, but he sneered at her efforts. He threw open the door and shoved her inside, slamming the door shut behind them.

Samantha had not known terror like this since the kidnapping that had brought her here. Frantically she beat at him, twisted away, and tried to plant a slim-heeled boot on his foot. All the while her heart slammed like a wild thing trapped in a cage as Pike held her by one wrist, fury flaring brightly in the depths of his small black eyes.

"I didn't do anything!" Samantha protested, hating herself at the same time for her pitiful weakness in the face of such a monster.

"Maybe you didn't. I don't give a damn what you actually did! But you betrayed me. You *betrayed* me! You bitch! You think you're so much better than the rest of us. You're not. And you'd better learn to play by my rules or not at all!"

"How did I betray you? How!? What did I do?" Samantha screamed, her brain racing in an attempt to determine the best way to calm him, to quell this storm that threatened to overwhelm her.

"You think I'm a fool?"

You're far worse than that, thought Samantha, but she remained mute.

"You're mine, and I'm gonna make sure nobody ever forgets that again."

Samantha could think of nothing but stopping this torture by whatever means. And like a cornered wildcat she clawed and pushed against Mississippi. Unexpectedly she broke free and reeled across the room where her heel caught in the braided rug. She nearly fell but recovered herself. Her breath came fast; her body trembled. She stood on the far side of the room, panting like a hunted animal, searching vainly for an avenue of escape. Mississippi stood planted, blocking

161

the door, a wicked leer smeared across his face which was wreathed in sweat. She eyed the side window but knew she could never jump to the alley. She remembered that Red Grissom was down in the saloon, but what were the chances of him venturing up here? Red was no gunman. Why would he risk his own life to save hers? Wasn't that what she herself had thought when she had found herself back in town with the unsuspecting peddler? Better his hide than hers?

The admonition of her mother ran through her head: *No one is ever going to help you, Sammy, so you gotta learn to help yourself.*

Mississippi began to take a step toward her, leering at her, taunting her. Samantha remained still. As he reached out to grab her, something like a dam bursting before the weight of too much water gave way in her. She dodged sideways and lunged for the door. Her fingers were on the latch, in the act of pulling it open when Mississippi's large brown hand reached above her head, abruptly snapping the door shut. He backhanded her with his free hand, dealing a blow that sent her reeling backwards along the wall for several steps. Her teeth tore the inside of her cheek, and she tasted the metallic, coppery flavor of her own blood. Her lip throbbed at the corner where it had split; blood dribbled down her chin.

Cold and detached, Mississippi followed her, hitting her again and again in rapid succession. The wounds along his arm and shoulder, marked by flecks of blood, did nothing to slow him.

Bright lights exploded behind Samantha's eyes as she stumbled away, animal instinct driving her to try to evade him, but to no avail. Nowhere in the room was there a hole small enough for her to crawl into that could provide protection from those cruel and brutal hands, hands that never failed to reach her again and again until the blows all ran together in a throbbing blur.

As if from a distance she heard the low, continuous swearing of a man accompanied by the voice of a woman, soft and whimpering. Was that the sound of her own voice? Surely it couldn't be! Yet it *was* her voice, pathetic and pleading. She began to collapse, no longer possessing the strength to try to elude the unavoidable any longer.

She collapsed to the floor beside the bed. Pike continued to vent his anger, although he changed his tactic to one of kicking. In the ribs, in her stomach, against her legs. Samantha fought the desire to surrender, to succumb into unconsciousness where sanctuary beckoned, but she resisted the urge. Instead, from her deepest inner resources she allowed the rage to build up inside her. This was not the time for self-hatred or self-pity. If he did not kill her, she *would* kill him. She would find a way to kill Mississippi Pike! She desperately clung to consciousness, waiting for her chance. Above the roaring in her ears she made her resolve. She would be alert enough to see it and strong enough to take it.

She was dimly aware of Mississippi, towering over her, and of a voice calling out to him from the hall beyond the door. The voice was familiar, but she could not gather enough of her senses to put a face to it. She only knew that it was another of Crockett's men, and that there would be no help for her from that quarter.

Mississippi answered the caller from where he stood with a gruff shout that seemed to shake the very walls of her room. Then he bent down low over her and grasped her chin roughly with one hand while the other encircled her neck.

"You stay right here and think about this," he sneered softly in her ear. "I'm not done with you yet. When I get back, we'll continue this lesson."

Samantha did not move. She was not sure that she could have moved if she had tried, but, as long as Mississippi was still in the room, she dared not make such an attempt. It was better to let him think she was too weak to escape. If he thought her capable of independent movement, he might have the man outside the door keep watch, or worse yet tie her up.

Mississippi stared down at her for long seconds, reveling in his power over her, then he turned on his heel and left, closing the door loudly behind him.

Samantha groaned. She could hear the two men talking outside the door. Then there was silence, save for the sound of retreating footsteps. She was alone.

An awesome silence settled over the room, offering a calming wave to the din that pounded in Samantha's head. She opened her eyes which felt tender and swollen. The room was a mass of undulating images before it came slowly into focus. As she raised her head, propping herself on an elbow, sharp pains lanced through her body. The taste of blood, sharp and salty, filled her mouth. She became aware that the odd, sporadic rasping sound was her own breathing. She was gasping, almost gulping air.

Samantha shuddered, the odd rhythm of her own ragged breathing filling the room. One thought rooted itself in her befuddled mind. She had to get away before Mississippi returned. She pulled herself upright by leaning heavily against the edge of the bed. The room swam away from her in dark swirls. For several moments Samantha hovered close to unconsciousness. Panic sliced through her, but determination held her upright. Swaying, she gritted her teeth and held herself rigid until the room stopped tilting away from her and then inched her way to the wardrobe only a couple of steps away. She grabbed the first day clothes with which her hands came in contact. She made her way back to the bed and slowly, painfully, drew the clothes on with trembling hands, letting what she wore, torn in several places by Mississippi's yankings, fall to the floor.

She had to get away from the saloon, find shelter somewhere. But where? No one in Saquarra would hide her from Mississippi Pike. No one maybe, except Kane. Was there no one else? Then she thought of Kane's wagon. At least she could rest there, and the desire to sleep was overwhelming.

Samantha lurched unsteadily to her feet and braced herself. She made her way to the door. She edged slowly out into the hall with tiny, halting steps and toward the stairs that led down into the saloon. She remembered the back outdoor stairway and determined it was the best way to remain unseen by those inside.

In her dizzy and weakened state, looking down into the alley from the top of the stairs, the descent seemed impossible to her. As she stared, the stairs and ground below appeared to be heaving up and down, back and forth. She closed her eyes for a second and drew in a deep breath. She gripped the top rail with both hands and carefully eased herself down the stairs, one painful step at a time. She paused often, overwhelmed with vertigo. But she was driven on by the fear of being beaten again by Mississippi.

When she reached the bottom of the stairs, she paused again, squinting against the intense brightness of the day, her eyes grating in their sockets as if surrounded by sand. To move ahead she was going to have to relinquish her hold on the corner post of the wooden banister. Then, with jerking steps that swung from the knees instead of the hips and half doubled-over in pain, she started across the alley, heading for the backs of the buildings that lined the main street.

Samantha shuffled along, pushing aside thoughts of rest until she could make it to the wagon. *Would Kane be at his wagon?* she wondered. All she wanted to do was to rest, to lie down somewhere, to sleep, and the thought propelled her mechanically forward. Then she remembered that Kane and the others had been attempting to arrest Crockett. *Had they? If they had, were they all at the jail?*

Moving slowly, but with more determination now, she worked her way along the rear of the buildings. She knew what she had to do. She used her right hand to guide her by sliding it along the rough, weathered wood of the back walls of the buildings. Somehow she managed to keep herself from falling, pausing when a new surge of dizziness tempted to spin the world away from her.

Samantha finally reached the back of the livery. Using the corral railings for support, she started forward, knowing she risked being seen. The wagon was in sight, but more importantly the jail was near. So very near. She should rest now.

Sinking to her knees on the hard-packed earth, Samantha intended only to rest for a moment, but in that moment, when she let her resistance down, unconsciousness washed over her in a wave. Her grip on the cross bar of the corral relaxed, and she slid gently to the ground beside the wagon.

CHAPTER
FIFTEEN

Sheriff Clive Brown was first to go through the door into the jail. He walked straight through the office, stopping only for the keys to the cells. He was putting the key into the lock of one cell door and flinging it open as the peddler and his companion followed him through the front door. Kane still had his Winchester hooked beneath Crockett's chin. El Diablo brought up the rear, shotgun effectively covering their backs until the heavy wooden door was slammed and the crossbar put in position. Without a word they walked Crockett to the nearest cell, locked him in.

The sheriff strode immediately to his desk, throwing open the bottom drawer and extracting a nearly full bottle of whiskey along with three glasses. He sloshed whiskey into one, tossed it back, and thumped the leaded glass back on the desktop, looking from El Diablo to Kane.

"I been in a few gun scrapes in my time, boys, but the two of you handled them guns faster than you can spit and holler 'howdy.' Never been in such a powder-burnin' contest."

Kane closed the shutters over the front window and flipped their crossbar into place. Then he began to reload his rifle. "You didn't do too poorly yourself, Sheriff," he said, a smile interrupting his concentration for a brief moment.

"Hah!" was Clive Brown's only response, and then his attention shifted from Kane to El Diablo for whom he felt a new respect. "I held my own, but you two, hell, it was the stuff they write them damned dime novels about."

Kane closed another pair of shutters. "I hope not."

El Diablo eyed the shutters, a sweat of a different sort than that from exertion appearing on his brow. The room was beginning to feel smaller by the minute. His gaze became dark as he quavered, the shudders threatening to sough through limbs and body. He pasted a devilish, taunting grin on his face that had earned him his nickname and thumped the stock of the scatter-gun to the floorboards. "Do not be too hasty, *amigo mio*. Fame ees not such a bad thing."

The sheriff grunted. "You boys got some kind of a plan? Beyond this point, I mean."

Sheriff Brown was concerned with the safety of his town. There were admitted risks in what they were doing, and he had known that going in. Nonetheless, he had thrown in his lot with this crazy tin-pan man and his Mexican friend, and now there was the question of what happened next.

Kane shrugged as he moved about the room, checking the stoutness of the jail — windows and doors that could be used from the outside to gain access or, if necessary, provide a fast exit for those on the inside.

"I'm thinking about it," he conceded as if it were of secondary importance to him.

Sheriff Brown swore in a reverent whisper, but neither Kane nor El Diablo paid any attention.

The outlaw was staring up at the ceiling as Brown lowered himself into his chair, the creak, once his full weight was settled, startlingly loud in the jail's stillness. El Diablo's jump, like a nervous cat at the noise, drew a dry chuckle from Crockett where he sat unconcerned on the bunk in the cell.

"A little nervous?" Crockett directed his question at El Diablo. "Probably have a good reason to be."

El Diablo grappled with the strange, squeezing sensation generated by being confined in a small space. Then he forced a slow smile. "No more than you, señor, considering your segundo would much rather see you dead than out again."

Crockett's jaw snapped shut, and his eyes blazed.

El Diablo walked the wooden planks to Crockett's cell and directed his swiftly collecting venom at Crockett. "A wise man knows when to keep his own council," he said in the thickening silence. "How wise are you, Crockett?"

He turned away from the man in the cell and walked to the other side of the room where Kane was securing another window. He directed his attention to the back door as the sheriff, now having risen, moved to slide another heavy crossbar into place. A blistering sheen of sweat covered his face now as his eyes traveled from one barred window to the next and then to the doors and walls which all seemed to be closing in on him and

170

the center of the room. To distract himself he looked up at the ceiling, and there he saw a neatly cut square in its center. A trap door!

"That goes to the roof, does it not?" He changed his tact as smoothly as another man blinked.

"Sure does," Brown agreed, "though I don't think it's been open since the Indians raided Saquarra."

Indian raids. That explained a lot. The jail was built like a fort. The building itself was built of stout wood and massive timbers, with the outer walls extending upwards well above where the heavy beams lay cross-ways in support of the roof. From the outside notches were visible every few feet, obviously gun ports, and it was the highest building in town except for the hotel.

"This jail was designed to stand up under siege," El Diablo said evenly, already feeling a sense of release from the room's closeness as he picked up an old broom and began poking at the trap door.

Kane joined El Diablo in his effort, pulling up a chair for El Diablo to stand on as he announced: "We should be finding out just how well it does hold up under siege pretty soon now."

"His men are gonna come for him," Sheriff Brown remarked, jerking his thumb in Crockett's direction, the timbre of his voice honing a sharp edge.

El Diablo used the broom handle to push the trap door, until the seal of grime and time's passage gave way and the door flipped open with a dusty thud that shook the rafters and sent a shower of grit down on his head and scattering on the floor around him.

"There ees no doubt they'll come," he agreed with an enthusiastic toss of his head. "That ees what we are waiting for."

Dust was still sifting down into the room through the trap door when El Diablo stretched his arms to catch the edge of the opening the door had revealed and hauled himself up, rolling out of sight. His footsteps thudded softly overhead as he made his way to the front of the jail overlooking the quiet street, pointing straight as an arrow at Mex-town.

The cool freshness of the morning air struck him full in the face. The underlying chill made him smile despite the fact he knew it would soon be hotter than the underside of a saddle blanket. He breathed deeply, filling his lungs as a man long without water might fill his belly. His eyes swept from horizon to horizon, skimming past the town that lay at his feet. He could feel the terrible black tension slipping away, his breath returning to its normal rhythm. He cursed his own weakness even as he recovered from it, remembering back to another time.

The *rancho* was large, the *hacienda* plush. Descanso was seven. His young mother, Polonia, widowed only a short time before, had come to work in the big house. Not that her state of matrimony would have made any difference to the old Lion of Sonora, as the *patrón* liked to call himself. Polonia, with her dancing sloe eyes, her raven hair that shone in the sunlight like a dark river, and fresh, young face, had caught his attention while she had been working in the fields which fed the peons. She had been moved to the main house later that same day with promises of an easier life, tending to the big man's needs.

Polonia had gone willingly, happily, without a thought, taking her young son along with her.

"You be a big boy, Descanso," Polonia said as they approached the front door of the *hacienda*, his hand in hers. "This job will make things better for us. It is important that you be very good."

Descanso nodded solemnly, removing his hand from hers. He stood proudly beside her, a small replica of his dead father, when the door swung open.

Don Francisco, the Lion of Sonora, black-maned and brown-eyed, looked down at them from his majestic height. His face indicated approval when his eyes lit on Polonia which quickly changed to severe annoyance at the sight of the well-scrubbed, quiet little boy at her side.

"I could not leave him," Polonia hastened to explain. "He will be no trouble, *patrón*, I give you my word."

The look of disgust on his large, angular face softened with each one of her words.

"Come inside. Maria will show you your new duties."

With a joyful heart Polonia began her new job, enthusiastically polishing the silver candlesticks Don Francisco had scattered throughout his beautiful house, baking the bread with love in her heart for the kindness he had shown her, scrubbing the tiled floors on her knees and never getting tired.

"You are beautiful, Mama," Descanso piped at the end of the long day in his childish joy at her newly found contentment.

"You are beautiful," Don Francisco, who seemed to appear out of nowhere, echoed the child's sentiments. "Too beautiful to return to that mud shack when you can remain here . . . with me."

Polonia caught his meaning immediately. Her skin appeared infused with blood rushing to it, and her drooping shoulders stiffened.

"I am sorry. I cannot."

Taking Descanso by the hand, Polonia tried to step around the don and leave. He was too fast for her and blocked their exit.

"You can, Polonia. In fact, I'm afraid you *must*."

"No, *señor*, I am not that kind."

"You are no different from the others. You belong to me."

"Please, *señor*, I cannot."

"Mama?" Descanso questioned, sensing the sudden change in the atmosphere.

Ignoring the boy, Don Francisco took Polonia by the arms, dragging her up against him with brutal force which brooked no resistance.

But resist him she did, trying to pull away, fighting the superiority of his strength.

The Don held fast, lips curling in amusement at her struggles. "Did you think I brought you up here just to scrub my floors? Anyone can do that! The boy can do that! You are shy, and I find that attractive, but you are no blushing virgin, so do not try my patience with this act!" He shook her for emphasis as he spoke. "Do we go to my bed or do I take you, like a *puta*, on the floor you just scrubbed?"

Polonia shrieked, stamping her slim, sandaled foot ineffectually against his booted one. "It makes no difference, for that is what you will make me!"

174

Descanso tried to press between them, pounding small fists against Don Francisco's tree-trunk thighs. A stray blow caught the don directly between his legs. With a howl of pain and fury he tossed the boy aside like a cub. He stood for several agonizing moments before turning to go after Descanso who was crawling away from the horrible display.

"No!" Polonia cried out, clutching at Don Francisco's clothing, trying to protect her son.

But he was not to be deterred. He grabbed the cowering boy, threw him in a nearby closet, and locked the door.

Quietly crying and frightened, Descanso heard everything from inside that closet. His mother's soft pleas and cries. The unmistakable crack when she was slapped. Descanso was frantic to help his mother. He yelled until his high child's voice cracked and disappeared, beat on the door until both hands were bloody, but there was no escape from the tiny confines of the dark closet or the sound of his mother's pain.

He spent the remainder of the night and the following day locked in the closet with nothing to eat or drink. He soiled himself and was ashamed. Finally, late that night, after he had been forced to endure his mother's cries again, he was allowed out.

Polonia's face was bruised and swollen, tears streaking her cheeks when she embraced her son and led him from the closet. Don Francisco was towering behind her. From that time forward, Descanso was forced to come to the big house with his mother. Sometimes he would be locked in the closet immediately upon his arrival and left there through the day and night. Other times he would be expected to play as if he were any normal boy until sometime later he would be thrust into the closet, the lock snapping home as the don's arm encircled his mother and he planted a kiss on her mouth. All the joy drained out of his mother at the hands of Don Francisco. She smiled less and less frequently, and then only at Descanso.

The years passed, and Descanso grew toward manhood without Don Francisco's notice. When he was fifteen, though he was still much smaller than the towering giant of the don, Descanso armed himself with a butcher knife from the kitchen and ended his mother's years of torture, nearly cutting the cruel man's head from his shoulders.

After that, Descanso got himself a good horse from the corrals and rode out with half of Sonora trying to catch him for his crime. He had never seen his mother again.

El Diablo shook off the painful memory, eyes hardening as they swept the length of the main street, spotting what had drawn him from his musings. There was someone down there, creeping up on the jail.

"Hey, El Lobo," El Diablo's voice drifted down to them inside the jail, "we have company."

Kane gave the sheriff a knowing look, then crawled up on the desk he and Clive had centered under the trap door after El Diablo had gone up on the roof. He lifted himself up through the trap door and rolled himself onto the roof. "Keep an eye on our prisoner," he called down before uprighting himself.

Careful not to silhouette himself above the battlements, Kane moved quickly across the roof, pressing himself up against the rough wood that enclosed the roof like a parapet surrounding a fort, and had himself a look. The heat of the sun was quickly intensifying on the exposed roof as his gaze took in the sight of a shape sprawled in the dust near his peddler's wagon. There was the flutter of brown skirts in the morning breeze, an arm outstretched, and the unmistakable flow of long, blonde hair, shimmering in the glaring sunlight like polished gold.

"Samantha," El Diablo voiced Kane's thought. "The hair," he added, "a man cannot mistake that hair for anyone else's."

Kane nodded in agreement. "It's her. What do you think?"

El Diablo shrugged. "A trap? Bait, perhaps." He grinned. "I would be most glad to go out and bring her back. Then we will all know."

Kane rubbed his chin, where the beginning bristles of a beard itched, and glanced again in Samantha's direction. She wasn't moving. If she were bait, then it was not willingly.

"No, my friend," he said quietly to El Diablo's offer, "this one is mine. Cover me, if you can. If you can't, bring flowers to my grave, *amigo*."

El Diablo gave a short laugh, as Kane disappeared again inside the jail, and turned his attention back to the woman sprawled in the dust. No one was staked out near her that he could see, and she was well in the open. If someone were keeping an eye on her, it would have to be from the livery. El Diablo drew his six-gun and waited.

"He stayin' up there?" Brown asked Kane as he dropped onto the floor from the desk.

"I think he likes it better up there," Kane responded, drawing his gun from his holster.

"No foolin'! Some folks ain't got the brains to be hoss thieves, but I ain't one of 'em. Saw him getting himself squinched up as a prune in here. What's his problem?"

"Didn't ask. 'Sides, he can see things up there we can't down here. Cover me, Sheriff, we've got company out back."

Sheriff Brown hefted the scatter-gun left behind by El Diablo and moved to the door. "Company out back, huh? Guess it doesn't hurt to have him up there . . . I didn't see nothin'."

"Unless it's me or Samantha Cameron, blast anybody coming through the door with that thing. I don't like it, but I reckon you better leave it unbarred until I get back."

The door was solid with no window. If there were trouble out there, Kane needed to be able to get back inside the jail in a hurry. It might be just what Crockett's men were counting on. Yet, there had not really been time since the three had left the saloon with Crockett for Pike and the others to organize any kind of a rescue attempt. Maybe Samantha had managed to find trouble on her own. He wouldn't know for sure about anything until he reached her.

Kane slipped out the door and paused in the shaded shelter of the building. He had been to the jail only twice since his arrival in Saquarra. Cover between himself and Samantha was almost nonexistent. Once he reached the livery's corral, he would be less visible if he moved inside the fence rails. Between the jail and corral he could only stick close to the back walls. He flexed the arm that had been wounded in the knife fight. It was stiff and sore, but the wound had not been serious.

He thought of El Diablo on the roof top above him as he left the shelter of the jail's back wall and sprinted across the open to the livery's doors. He ducked behind one, dust rising from beneath the soles of his boots. He paused there, gun drawn, and sighted along the crack in the door. Nothing stirred inside. The livery was empty.

He covered the distance to the corral in four long strides, vaulting easily over the top rail. Inside, he kept himself low, moving easily between the few horses that occupied it.

Kane's golden eyes narrowed as he approached Samantha. Her head was turned away from him, but she was breathing. Nothing appeared to be wrong. Her hair shimmered in the morning sunlight. It was as if she had stretched out on the dusty ground for a short nap.

That familiar prickle raced up the back of his neck. Kane nudged Samantha, knowing he stood out in stark relief against the dun color of the dusty earth. She didn't respond.

Swearing softly, he holstered his six-gun and eased her over onto her back, cradling her head against his legs as he knelt beside her. The sight of her face made him wince. Bloodied and bruised, dusty and swollen, she was nearly unrecognizable. He swore again.

Samantha stirred and gave a small muffled moan, as though she knew it was not wise to make any loud noises. Her eyelids were bruised and swollen, the left one especially. She stared steadily up into his face, not appearing to be the least bit surprised that he was there.

"Do you make a habit of this?" he asked, finding himself at a loss for words as he studied her battered face.

Samantha smiled pathetically. "I sure do need a lot of saving these days," she whispered, her mouth and throat very dry and tight.

"Can you walk?" he asked gently.

Samantha winced, breathing hard with the effort to speak. "Haven't since I fell. But I got this far."

"Let's give it a try." he said. With gentle hands he lifted her up, supporting her about the waist. Again she winced. As she tottered upright, the world spun crazily away from her at the sudden movement, but she managed to regain her balance by holding still and taking in deep breaths for several seconds. They moved next to the fence.

Kane slid beneath the bottom rail, righted himself, and glanced around. Then he carefully eased her after him, trying to keep her head and shoulders lifted clear of the rocky ground. Samantha breathed deeply, focusing her efforts on not crying out.

"I can walk," she whispered once they cleared the fence. "Help me up again."

"Lean on me," Kane recommended as he slipped his arm around her back and tried to shift her weight to his side and leg. "Let me do the work."

Samantha allowed herself to be carried along by him, shuffling her leaden feet in feeble assistance. They moved in tandem, doubled over in a tight crouch. He was pushing her faster than perhaps he should, but there was no predicting Mississippi Pike. He did not want to be cut off from the jail when the man decided to move.

Samantha stumbled. Kane swung her up into his arms and carried her the last few yards to the door. It swung open before them, and Kane whisked her inside, relieved as the sound of the wooden bar rasped against the wooden door into its metal brace. He passed the sheriff in the narrow passageway and headed for the first cell and the cot it provided.

Frank Crockett sat up from sprawling on his cot to take a keen interest in this latest addition to the jail. He watched as Kane carried Samantha into the cell, laying her gently on the narrow bunk.

"You really *are* crazy," he observed, now standing and leaning with casual ease against the cold bracing of the cell's bars. "Any man who would do what you just did with half the town ready to come down on his back like an Apache war party *has* to be out of his mind." Crockett's cool, amber eyes shifted to Samantha, but he continued to address Kane. "The Mex is as insane as you are. And he can't stand closed-in places. How's he going to handle it when things get hot?"

"Don't plan on thinkin' about it much," was Kane's aggravated reply. "Seems he likes the roof. No concern of yours."

Kane left the cell to get a basin of water and a clean cloth from the sheriff's stores. He returned to where Samantha was stretched out under the watchful eye of Frank Crockett.

The town boss grimaced with a shrug. "I'm a little crazy myself. In fact," he went on as the peddler began gently bathing the woman's battered face, "the only sane ones here are probably the sheriff and that woman."

Carefully Kane sponged away the dried blood and caked dust from her face. The bruising was substantial, but for the most part there would be no major physical scars, though he could say nothing about the other, more lasting kind. Her lips were split in several places. As he cleansed her face, he uncovered one rather deep cut above her left eyebrow, and the swelling of her nose suggested it might be broken.

"Hey, El Lobo, what've we got?" El Diablo called down from the roof, head thrust through the trap-door opening.

"Trouble," the peddler responded.

El Diablo chuckled, the sound soft and menacing. "That ees no more than we already had. I'm watching the street."

"You could end this quickly," Crockett interjected at this point. "Just let me go and walk away from this. I'll give you safe passage out of Saquarra if you promise never to return."

Kane was nearly finished with his work. He glanced up at Crockett and cocked an eyebrow. "Not interested," he said amiably. Kane then went to replace the dirty water in the basin. When he returned, he laid the wrung-out cloth across Samantha's swollen eyes. Then he added in delayed response to Crockett: "I've had myself a look around. I'm going to stay."

Samantha clutched at his sleeve, licking her lips which no longer tasted of blood. "Don't be a fool, Kane," she got out, her voice barely audible. "Just get out before you get yourself killed."

Samantha's throat was dry, and there was that overwhelming desire to sleep pulling at her. Kane held a glass of water to her lips. It hurt to have the rim of the glass pressed ever so gently against her lips, but the cool water tasted good. She drank thirstily, ignoring the droplets that dribbled onto her bodice.

Kane watched her. Having her here meant even more trouble for them. But he knew she was an outcast among the citizens of Saquarra as she would be in most places where they knew her history. If not here, where then would she be safe from the hands of Mississippi?

"We gonna go after Pike?" Brown asked Kane, deferring to him for leadership.

Kane went to the front window and opened the wooden shutter. His eyes fell on the delegation of Saquarra's citizens approaching the jail almost at the same instant that El Diablo signaled to him from the roof with a couple of loud thumps of his boot. Brown joined him at the window.

"Not right now," Kane murmured thoughtfully.

CHAPTER
SIXTEEN

Crockett quickly became interested in what was going on outside the jail. His eyes glittered as he strode across his cell to get a better view out the window. The boards creaked beneath his footfalls. "They didn't waste any time, did they?" he asked of no one in particular.

"What do we have out there, Clive?" Kane asked, staring toward the gathering crowd.

"They're all local," the sheriff answered tersely, his gaze fixed on the clutch of humanity congregating outside his jail.

All of them were people he knew. Men he had shared beers with at the saloon. Now they ringed the front of the jail like a pack of winter-starved wolves. Their faces were grim, set, and a stiff coolness emanated from the crowd. Finally, when they halted their steady advance on the jail, one of their number stepped forward. It was Harlan Moody, the bartender. He had always been one of Crockett's strongest supporters in Saquarra.

"Sheriff!" Moody called out gruffly, "open up! Folks here've got a bone to pick, an' they asked me to do the talkin' for 'em."

"Recognize any of Crockett's men out there?" asked Kane

The sheriff didn't have a chance to reply before Crockett broke in. "Won't need my men. The good citizens of Saquarra are going to set you straight. And I think you're going to reconsider and let me walk out of here before this whole town comes down around your ears."

The sheriff glanced questioningly at Kane. "Think we ought to let him in?"

Kane shrugged. "Go ahead, let him in. We'll hear what he has to say."

"Come ahead," Sheriff Brown called. "Just Moody, though. The rest of you stay where you are. I don't want any trouble here."

"You better come down," Kane called up to El Diablo. "We want him to see us all together, not wonder where one of us got to."

Moving quickly, the Mexican bandit swung down and closed the trap door after him. He sauntered over to where he could keep a casual eye out the window, both to watch the crowd and to keep at bay that oppressive, strangling sensation caused by his claustrophobia.

Kane was glad El Diablo closed the trap door leading to the roof. It was probably something everyone in Saquarra knew about but might have forgotten. No need to remind them.

Sheriff Brown lifted the bar from the front door, opening the door just wide enough to admit Moody. After he had entered, the door was slammed shut and the bar dropped back into place.

"What the hell do you think you're doing to this town, Clive?" Moody demanded as soon as the bar was down. "You brought in a gunman, you son of a bitch."

Kane shook his head in wonderment. Frank Crockett had this town by the throat. Some knew it; some were dumb enough to believe otherwise; and others did not care. But no matter what their view, they were all out there, grimly set against change.

Judging from the way Moody handled himself, Kane was willing to bet Moody had appointed himself spokesman for the people of Saquarra. He was a spare man, this bartender, yet he cast a pretty good shadow. It was his eyes, narrow and shifty, and the set of his face that Kane did not like. The man was a back biter, and he would bear close watching.

"You're supposed to keep the peace in this town, Sheriff, not start a war," Moody ground out viciously. "You can bet Crockett's men are going to tear this town down to get him out of here."

"The man is responsible for a lot of the robbing and killing of people that goes on out there," Clive spit out as he gestured toward Crockett, "but you say it's okay, as long as it's somebody else. He's wringing the life out of this town with his form of 'protection.' He's no better than the vultures he's keeping out of this town, and what about the ones he lets in? He's getting rich off the men who come here to hide out. As long as we protect them in Saquarra, we're responsible for what they do before they come here and after they leave. I say it's not right, never has been, and now I'm backing these two who want to stop him in every way I can. If you had any sense, you'd do the same."

Out of the corner of his eye Kane saw Crockett leaning casually against the bars of his cell, watching with all the disinterest of a bystander observing a family squabble.

"Then you're fired, Clive. You ain't sheriff here any more." Moody spoke with an ill-concealed sneer. "And you," he turned to Kane, swelled with his own importance, "you can take your friend there and clear out of Saquarra by sundown."

The planes of Kane's face flattened and angled, pulled by cold fury. His golden eyes caught and held the officious wire of a man while he contained his anger.

"I don't think so," he said with deadly calm, "and, if you or anyone else gets in my way, I'll blow your head off."

"I share the sentiment," Brown said flatly. "I've got fliers on the man. If you try an' stop me, I'm within my rights to shoot you down."

Moody colored bright crimson, and his cheeks puffed out. He was plainly preparing for some monumental bluster, but Crockett took the opportunity to intervene.

"Stay out of it." Crockett directed his remark at the bartender. "Let my boys handle it, and no one'll get hurt, except maybe the men in this room. We're not looking for bloodshed here. Maybe, if they know when to quit, we'll just run 'em on out of town."

El Diablo burst out laughing. "He ees a very funny man," he said to the room at large. He continued to chuckle, eyes tightening at the corners. His eyes found Crockett, and he humbly stated: "You will have to forgive me, señor, but I believe you are lying."

Crockett shrugged, indicating his disinterest.

Samantha, who had been stirring on her cot, presently sat up, lifting her face in Moody's direction. She said: "Don't be a fool, Moody. If you people pull together, you can be a real town again. Maybe a good place to live and raise kids."

Upon seeing her battered face, Moody became noticeably disturbed. He turned his attention to the floor near his feet. "Saquarra is just fine the way it is," he stated loudly, then let his gaze move to the town's despot. His tone adjusted to one of respect when he addressed the big man. "All right, Mister Crockett, we'll do as you say and keep clear of it for now. I'll tell the others."

"You do that," Crockett said evenly. "And tell Mississippi to hurry up."

Moody nodded solemnly to Crockett, then sidled to the door like a damned desert sidewinder. Kane did not believe the barkeep meant what he said to Crockett — that he would stay out of it and tell the others to do the same. He was basking in the great man's presence. He had determined that the best way to benefit himself was to spring Frank Crockett.

Moody was, in fact, determined to do just that, not lurk in the background while the matter was settled without him. He was too filled with self-importance. As

188

Moody stood at the door waiting for someone to lift the crossbar, Kane approached him.

"How many of Crockett's men are in town now?" he demanded, although he didn't expect a straight answer. He knew it was possible to tell as much from what a man did not say as from what he did. Moody did not let him down.

"Enough, tin-pan man, to make wolf meat out of all of you."

Kane did not delay Harlan Moody's departure any longer. It would have been just as easy to throw the man in the cell with Frank Crockett as to let him go, but he doubted that such an action would change anything, and he certainly didn't want to listen to the bartender's harangue until this was over.

Sheriff Brown slid the heavy cross-timber in place across the door as Kane moved to the window to watch Moody's departure.

"Well," Kane asked of his companions, "what do you think?"

"I think they're gonna try an' tear down this meat house, an' it's gonna be right soon," Brown said roughly.

El Diablo chuckled without comment. The cramped quarters of the jail threatened to bring on a shudder he would be hard pressed to conceal. "I think I will follow the example of the puma and seek again the high places." He jumped on the desk to open the trap door. He fastened a sympathetic gaze on Samantha before boosting himself up, and then hastily disappeared.

Samantha sat quietly in the cell. She didn't feel safe, and it was becoming apparent that no one in Saquarra

189

did. Holding the wet cloth over her left eye, she forced herself to remain alert, focusing her other eye on the peddler standing beside the window, his attention fixed on the street outside. The sheriff's allegiance to Kane surprised her since she had never judged the man to have enough guts to go up against Frank Crockett and his boys out in the open. She was glad there was now no sign of the Mexican who made her skin crawl. She nearly jumped off the cot when her musing was interrupted by the sound of a question directed at her.

"Mississippi?" the voice asked softly.

Samantha turned and stared questioningly at Frank Crockett who stood very near the bars shared by the two cells, speaking in barely audible tones.

"Did Mississippi do that to you?" Crockett asked the question, his amber eyes soft and seemingly filled with pity.

She nodded slowly.

Crockett let loose a string of oaths directed at Mississippi that startled Samantha with their power. In wide-eyed surprise she stared at him as he continued the barrage of oaths. He glanced at her again in the midst of his tirade. *Ahhh*, that was the response he had hoped to see on her face. After all, she was in an unlocked cell, and the others in the jail trusted her. If he could manage to convince her of his good intentions and manipulate her to his own ends, this fight would be won without a shot being fired.

"I'll take care of Mississippi when I get out of here. He's been getting too big for his britches for some time now. You know," his tone changed to one of unexpected gentleness as he looked her fully in the face, "I've admired you since the first time I saw you, Samantha." His tone was low, his words reaching the woman's ears alone. "Right now, you're in a very good position to help me, and, if you do, I'll be in a very good position to help you."

"I'm going to kill Mississippi," Samantha told him bluntly.

Crockett's broad, sun-browned face broke into a beguiling smile. "It's beginning to look like you're going to have to wait in line for that privilege," he whispered. "Others are ahead of you." Crockett nodded in Kane's direction. "Him for one and" — he paused — "me for another." He looked at her more seriously. "Help me when you see a chance, Samantha, and I'll get you out of Saquarra if that's what you want. I promise . . . it's the least I can do, considering what you've been through."

Samantha felt confused by his kind words. "Why should I trust you? You hired that scum."

"I realize my mistake. But Mississippi served a purpose . . . before." Crockett felt that with a little more prodding he could win her over to his side. He didn't have much time, but he knew he couldn't rush her. "Think about the people of Saquarra. This matter isn't worth shedding blood over. Taking care of Mississippi would change a lot of things. Just think about it for a while, Samantha. Give it some serious thought."

Samantha did not get a chance to answer. Kane had shifted his attention from the street to the cells. He was heading toward her. Thoughts tumbled through her mind as he approached with those same steady, even strides she remembered so well. It telegraphed a confidence no mere peddler should possess, but then he had already told her he had fought in the war. He was strong, opinionated, and willing to fight for what he believed in, but another simple fact stuck in her head. The words of her mother: *No one is ever going to help you, Sammy, so you gotta learn to look out for yourself.* She owed nothing to the strange, tall man with the golden wolf's eyes so penetrating they seemed capable of reading another's thoughts. Yet, in spite of the risk, he had rescued her a second time out there in the dust where she had fallen. Then again, she had not betrayed him to Mississippi, even if it had been done largely in an effort to protect herself.

She might have been wiser to have gone to Crockett a long time ago. Perhaps, even now, she should take the outlaw up on his offer and help him. She couldn't imagine the sheriff, showing sudden nerve, along with the peddler and that devil of a Mexican coming out of this alive. But Samantha Cameron was a survivor. She told herself again, she owed nothing to this tin-pan man.

Kane looked sharply at Crockett in the next cell, noting that the big man stood next to the bars nearest Samantha. He squatted on his heels before her. "You feeling better?"

"A little," she answered without meeting his eyes, afraid he was reading her thoughts and that he would know she had doubts about the outcome of this stand-off.

Glancing from Samantha to Crockett, Kane could guess what the man had been saying to her. Crockett wanted out of his cell and would reward handsomely anyone who helped him. Saquarra's town boss would be more than capable of protecting her against his *segundo*. In fact, it appeared Mississippi's usefulness to Frank Crockett was just about at an end. No fool, Mississippi would be reading the situation the same way.

If there was a way, Kane intended to use this fact to his advantage. He cocked his head, looking at the woman a little more closely.

"Do you need a doctor?"

Samantha shrugged, taking the moist cloth from her eye to dip it again into the basin of water. "No. Besides, the one who lives here spends more time out of town than in. Gives you something to think about when they're shooting at you," Samantha added with a wry smile that was lost in the bruised puffiness of her face.

"Got a couple of men ridin' out," Clive announced from his post beside the window as he peered through the cracked shutter.

"Crockett's men?" Kane asked.

The sheriff shook his head. "Couple of Saquarra's boarders. It appears they don't like the direction things are headed."

Kane joined him at the window and looked out. Dust rose in a plume, driven up by the departing riders. Several of Crockett's men were in a huddle outside the saloon, and the street was still filled with little knots of the town's citizens. Moody was drifting from one group to another like a sergeant rallying his troops before a battle. Guns bristled from all quarters as numerous as quills on a porcupine. The two that had ridden out would not do much to shift odds in their favor, but it was better than having two more ride in.

Hooking his foot around the leg of a chair, Kane dragged it up to the window and sat down, prepared to wait. Trouble, he decided, was apt to flow from more than one direction.

CHAPTER
SEVENTEEN

On the Mexican side of the deadline most of the citizens — women and children being no exceptions — were gathered in a run-down adobe with a wooden roof that served as the *cantina*.

"He is a crazy man, nothing more," one voice rose above the general murmur of the crowd. "And he is a stranger. He has been here only a few days."

"He is brave man," Aniceta Esquivel returned in a strong voice. "He treats us no differently than anyone else in Saquarra, and he has friends who have joined him."

"An outlaw and the sheriff. We all know what El Diablo is. And this peddler only wishes to make money. The sheriff, I think, he is tired of being under Crockett's thumb. The three of them do not make much of an army."

"It does not matter," Aniceta announced. "A small trickle can turn into a mighty river when a storm breaks. We are the storm, *amigos*. We must join this Zachariah Kane. Now is the time to rid Saquarra of Frank Crockett for good."

"Strong talk, Aniceta, but it is not you who will be expected to take up a gun."

"Then I will volunteer! My son would already be dead if not for Kane!"

Roberto, a very tall, slender young man, shook his head doubtfully. "Why should we worry about Saquarra? It is not so much our town. The *gringos* barely tolerate us. Crockett's men pay little attention to us. It is not our fight."

"Then whose?"

"Let the *gringos* fight the *gringos!*"

"You think a bullet will go around you because you live on this side of town instead of the other?"

"I think there will be fewer bullets here."

Aniceta tossed her head, black hair a shimmering curtain, dark eyes flashing. "Then you are truly a fool, Roberto."

She turned from him in disgust, slight frame rigid, shoulders squared, chin lifted. "What about the rest of you? Are you fools as well?"

There were a few mutterings and shufflings as the people in the room began to separate, parting into opposing camps. Some glowered at the small, determined woman; others avoided her fiery gaze. Then a new path was cut through the crowd as *Padre* Ramón passed among them like Moses parting the Red Sea. He was not a very tall man, but built solidly, with a square frame that made his brown cassock all the more imposing as he made his way to the front of the gathering.

"Do you think I am a fool, Aniceta? I do not take up arms and rush into the fray, nor do I advocate violence!"

She colored a little but did not back down from the priest. "We are not sheep, *Padre*. If we do not wish all we hold dear to be destroyed, we must take a stand now."

"Not with bullets."

"With anything we have!" Miguel Montoya said as he stepped forward, aligning himself with the small, feisty woman. "She is right!"

Padre Ramón's piousness took on an edge. "You speak of murder, my son."

"I speak of justice, *Padre!* Crockett is a thief and a murderer. We know that, and he squeezes Saquarra each day he is still here. If we wish to live without fear, Saquarra must rid herself of him."

A small child on the far side of the room began to cry. Another in a squeaky, high-pitched voice echoed the fear in that cry. Someone coughed, and before any more words could be exchanged, the *cantina's* front door opened.

Zeb Kraus, owner of the general store, entered with a quiet diffidence, dusty brown hat clutched between his hands. He crushed it even further when he realized a weighty silence had settled over the room and all eyes were fixed on him and his wife, Rosa, a plump, red-cheeked woman with flaxen hair, timidly following him inside.

"Excuse us, folks," Zeb said delicately. "We don't mean to interrupt, and we sure don't want to intrude, but, if I was a betting man, I'd say you were here talking about what the rest of Saquarra has been discussing for the past couple of hours."

197

Affirming murmurs filled the room.

"This town is a powder keg. Yes, sir, no doubt about it." He slapped his brown hat against his thigh for emphasis. "And the way I see it, the question is not when it will blow, but who's gonna light the fuse?"

Miguel stepped forward with Aniceta his shadow. "You tell us nothing we do not know. You say you do not wish to intrude, but you do. What is it you want?"

Aniceta placed a placating hand on his arm. "We must think, Miguel, not react. If I am right, we must work together." She turned to Zeb. "Am I right? Is that why you have come here?"

Zeb and Rosa shifted aside enough to allow Ben Ford, the stout and rumpled livery owner, to enter with his wife, Emily, a small, bird-like woman.

"I told you this wasn't such a good idea," Ben sputtered nervously as he glanced around the room, eyes slipping and sliding over the gathered crowd, not really focusing on any individual.

"Shut up, Ben," Emily chirped in a voice that piped through the crowd and brought smiles to one and all.

More of Saquarra's solid citizens edged their way in through the door, hesitant, faces solemn and strained. There was a sprinkling of single men, but most were married, accompanied by their wives and, in some cases, children.

The tension broken, Saquarra's two factions began to size up one another. Roberto gave a loud snort and stalked out.

"Well," Zeb said firmly, "I guess we know that's a true feeling on both sides of the line. We've got folks that aren't going to see things our way. So, since those men over in the jail are going to need help and I don't think any of us want to be shooting our neighbors, we've got some planning to do."

"Not if it includes raising weapons in the name of vengeance," the *padre* said, stepping out in front of his flock.

"*Padre,* we all know what we're here for," Aniceta overrode him. "You are welcome to stay, but we will do what we must."

In the meantime Miguel had stepped closer to the newcomers. He thrust his hand out to the storekeeper, and Zeb clasped it firmly in his large, meaty hand.

Mississippi Pike was in a fury that few had ever witnessed before. He had more than one reason since the news of Crockett's arrest had spread through Saquarra and some of the hangers-on had ridden out within the hour. Others had followed, realizing Crockett's reign was nearly at an end. The men were becoming unmanageable without guidance. They were all determined to get Crockett out of jail, but each one had a different idea as to how this would be best accomplished. They were peeling in different directions, and Pike was having a hell of a time pulling them together. That damned Roary Sikes was drawing off Pike's support.

Crockett's arrest was the opportunity Mississippi had been waiting for, and now he was losing precious time in trying to implement a plan to take over. Crockett would be broken out of jail all right, but, the way Pike saw it, the big man wasn't going to survive his rescue. The *segundo* planned on burning those bastards out of there. A dramatic stroke that Crockett's hardened men would most likely approve. That he was Crockett's lieutenant would weigh heavily in their decision to give up any independent action and join him in his plan. Mississippi had no doubt that, once they were all with him, Crockett's death would hardly be noticed, except as an excuse to finish off the tin-pan man and that Mex partner of his.

He stared hard at a small number of the town's local citizenry, standing uncertainly at the bar or sitting uncomfortably around the tables inside the saloon. Only the menfolk were at this meeting. Many scowled and glanced nervously at Mississippi. The rest didn't look any too sure about what they were doing here. Harlan Moody was back behind the bar, swaggering up a storm.

"I'm only gonna say this one time." Pike ground out his words and prowled the floorboards. "There's gonna be lead flyin' thick as flies in this town real soon. You better pick a side and stick with it, and it better be the right one. I'm tellin' you the winning side is with Frank Crockett."

"You bet it is!" Moody echoed Pike's sentiments.

"You-all know what he's done for this town! Now you owe him. He ain't gonna take kindly to those who don't back him after all he's done for you." As an afterthought Mississippi added ominously: "Neither will I, and, till Frank's out of that jail, *I'm* givin' the orders."

The silence in the room was thick as desert air in the midst of a dust storm. Then Moody's voice rang sharply in the silence.

"We're gonna back him, ain't we, boys? This town knows which side its bread is buttered on!"

There were a few grumbling dissenters, the sound of the shuffling of boots, followed by another period of troubled silence. As usual, Moody behaved like a stray dog — having licked Crockett's boots, now he was eyeing Pike's. He liked being the big man in town, bullying his fellow citizens. The man was not worth much, but there were times when he could be used to advantage. The rest of the townsfolk usually seemed to listen to him.

"Did anybody ride out to tell Buck Mitchell what's going on here?" a voice from out of the small, tight crowd asked.

"Mitchell's a rancher. He ain't got nothin' to do with this," Mississippi shot back.

"He will have if he comes riding into town with his boys and into a shoot-out," Saquarra's barber, Edgar Potter, announced. "Him and his pack tote a lot of guns. Enough to make a mark in a war."

"He didn't make much difference before Crockett got here."

"Yeah, but he's always defended his own," Potter offered by way of explanation. "Does a pretty good job of that."

Ignoring Potter, Pike turned to ask Moody: "Did you do what I asked you to do?"

Moody sidled up to the bar across from Mississippi and nodded. He held a beer in one hand and leaned his ham-like forearms on the highly polished wood. He didn't make much of an effort to keep his words private when he imparted his information.

"Mister Crockett's in the back cell. He seemed all right. He told me to keep out of it, though. He said you and the boys could handle things just fine. He also said to keep the rest of the townsmen out of it."

Almost in slow motion Mississippi reached out, grabbed a handful of Moody's shirt front, and shook him like a rat. "Now look" — he spit out the words between clenched teeth — "Crockett's in jail. He's liable to get himself killed before this thing is over. In the meantime you take your orders from me and keep your mouth shut."

Pike allowed the words to sink into Moody's brain before he relinquished his grasp on the bartender. Moody eased back to take a long pull on his beer as if nothing had happened.

The batwings snapped and flapped as Roary Sikes, boots thudding heavily on the wooden floor, entered the saloon. He looked right at Pike and gave a greasy smile.

"Got something cookin' over in Mex-town," he announced to Pike. "They're havin' themselves a meetin'."

Pike laughed. "So what? Ain't got a backbone betwixt the whole passel of 'em."

"I wouldn't be so sure about that. The way I heard it, some of the good folks of Saquarra have sauntered on over to join 'em."

202

"You're sure?" Mississippi snapped, his fury rising again in a new wave.

Sikes nodded.

"Then get some of the boys and go on over there and break it up! Are you stupid? Can't you do nothin' without bein' told direct?"

Roary Sikes dropped his hands to the butts of his pair of pistols, caressing them lovingly, staring hard at Crockett's *segundo*. He broke out into a smile.

"There's somethin' else you should know, Pike," Moody put in, trying to break the tension.

"And what's that?"

"Your girlfriend's over at the jail, too. In the cell right next to Crockett's. Only difference is she don't look too good, and her cell door ain't locked."

Mississippi's beady, obsidian eyes fastened on Moody and held. It didn't seem possible. Samantha had barely been able to move when he'd left her. How could she have gotten to the jail? Certainly no one in Saquarra had guts enough to help her. No one except . . . that damned peddler!

Pike's lip lifted in a feral snarl, but he remained silent for long seconds. When he spoke, it was to snap orders at Sikes. "Break up that damned meetin'. Now! Then get the boys together. I want everybody here . . . every man on Crockett's payroll. Bring in anyone in this town who owes Crockett. We're gonna have a meetin' of our own."

Without another word Mississippi turned from Sikes and started at a slow pace up the stairs to Samantha's room. He found her door slightly ajar. Her night dress and wrapper lay on the floor in the corner near her wardrobe, but she was nowhere in evidence. She had slipped away and gone straight to that tin-pan man.

The wooden walls vibrated with the resonance of Mississippi's vicious swearing. "Try and play me for a fool, woman! Then, dammit, pay the price!"

Abruptly he turned away from the hollow, mocking room and slammed the door with enough force nearly to rock it from its hinges. His eyes glittered, sparking black thoughts. When he got his hands on her again, he would kill her.

Pike headed down the stairs, taking two at a time, bootheels ringing, wood creaking a sharp protest. "Cullen! Jake!" he thundered as he descended, his glance passing over to the far end of the bar. "Mac!" He yelled, waiting for a response from any one of them, bellowing for his men the way Frank Crockett never did.

"Yeah?" Cullen asked as he stuck his head in through the batwings.

"Get the rest of the boys," Pike commanded. "We're gonna move."

"Sure thing!" Cullen's head disappeared around the corner. The rapid thud of retreating footsteps could be heard on the boardwalk outside.

"We're gonna hit 'em fast," Mississippi said to those remaining in the saloon, formulating the plan as he spoke. "We ain't even gonna get within range of them shootin' irons inside the jail. We're gonna burn it down."

A couple of the men hooted in glee. Pike strutted a few paces, tantalizing his audience. Anger puffed out his chest and put flames in his eyes. He was going to show them all, by God. He'd have them all crawling on their bellies when this was over.

Mac, one of Crockett's men, came bursting into the saloon, wild-eyed, looking for Pike. Spotting his quarry at the bar pouring himself a drink with a flourish, he hurried over to him.

"A couple of the boys are over to the jail tryin' to break Frank out. They're gonna . . ." His statement was interrupted by a flurry of gunshots echoing down the length of the street. They were coming from the direction of the jail.

"Who's doing this?" Mississippi demanded, jerking around at the sudden intrusion of the gunshots.

"Hank and Wes. Shouldn't we go give 'em a hand?"

Mississippi shook his head, "They're a couple of damn' idiots. If they pull it off, we'll give 'em a medal. If they don't, we'll bury 'em. I'm bettin' they don't make it. In the meantime I give the orders, and I say we go ahead with my plan. That one over to the jail's more of a curly wolf than we first give him credit for."

The flurry of shots ripping through the town sounded like a full-scale assault on a battlefield. It lacked only the thundering hoofs of charging horses and perhaps a bugle call. Then the flurry stopped as suddenly as it started, and a silence settled over the town. Occasionally single shots, even and well spaced, broke the silence along with another weapon — a heavier weapon, probably a rifle. It was the slow deliberateness of the shots that was even more distracting to Pike than the fusillade that had preceded them. Whoever was pulling that trigger was in no hurry. He was taking his time, lining up his shots — and a man shooting like that was not likely to miss very often. Pike turned that over in his mind and determined to keep well out of rifle range of the jail.

The gunfire had ceased, the sharp reports rolling off into the distance, echoes dying out on the still desert air like some distant ghostly battle drawing to a close. Mississippi and the assembled men now stood in the saloon, sipping whiskey. Pike's ear remained well tuned to the silence outside. The roar of the scatter-gun that had been used by the Mex in the saloon had not been discernible. The scatter-gun was a great equalizer, but that damned turn-coat Mex apparently was not fond of using the weapon. With this silence there settled over Saquarra a grim air of expectancy. The townsmen had vanished from the saloon.

Pike leaned on his elbows, braced against the bar. "Streets cleared?" he finally grumbled at Moody.

"Nothin' left but the dust."

"Don't surprise me none. Like rats lookin' for holes to climb into. What a brave bunch here in Saquarra. Kinda sorry I missed seein' 'em scatter."

The huge old clock on the wall behind the bar started gonging out the time when Cullen returned to the saloon, stampeding his way through the batwings. Several hardened men trailed along in his wake. All of them wore grim, expectant faces. Pike glanced at the clock. Two in the afternoon. The sun was high in its

206

climb across the sky. Heat rose in waves off the street outside. It was almost time to lay siege to the jail.

"They got Hank and Wes," Cullen reported angrily. "Nailed 'em both without hardly working up a good sweat."

"Hank and Wes were fools," Mississippi stated flatly. "I told everybody I was in charge. I told 'em not to do anything that wasn't a direct order from me. I said we'd get Crockett out of there. They didn't listen . . . now they're dead. They got what fools deserve."

"One of their men is up on the roof," Cullen said as he laid his rifle on the bar with a solid ring. He swore under his breath when Moody slopped a glass of beer in front of him.

"The roof!" Pike exploded, turning to face Cullen. "How the hell did one of 'em get up there without bein' seen?" His glower spread around the room, taking in all the men as if they had let him down.

"Trap door inside the jail," Moody volunteered from his place behind the bar.

"You could 'a' told me about that before!" Mississippi's temper flared again.

"Never thought of it." Harlan shrugged, though he blanched under the outlaw's attack. "The thing hasn't been used since you and Crockett came. I forgot about it."

"Anythin' else you didn't think to tell us?" Pike asked.

Moody looked a bit edgy beneath the close scrutiny of Crockett's lieutenant, but finally he nodded. "The hotel roof is higher. You put a man up there, you'll be able to pick off the man on the jail roof like shootin' fish in a barrel."

The hotel. There was one building between the jail and the hotel. As Mississippi considered the town's layout, he realized the hotel was the perfect place to position the men who would touch off the fire in the jail. He began to take stock of those still gathered in the saloon. There was Cullen, tough, fast, and equipped with a bull-headed stubbornness that never allowed him to quit. Mac, dark, slender, and slimy, who preferred a more round-about approach, was vicious as a badger when cornered. Jake was with them, and he didn't particularly care what he did so long as there was something to be gained by it. Bo, a man who always seemed to be lounging about but missed very little, chose to take orders because he had long ago decided it was easier to take them than to give them. Hinx and Calloway had ridden into Saquarra together, and both were unknown quantities, though they had rotten reputations which suited Pike just fine. They had obviously thrown in with Mississippi when he had put the word out that he was going to take the jail. Pete, another of Crockett's men, stood watch at the saloon's back door. He could be trusted.

From Pike's perspective he had an army between the men on Crockett's payroll and visiting outlaws not eager to lose their roost. He almost laughed out loud. It was going to be easy, and Frank Crockett was going to get the surprise of his life, just before he died.

CHAPTER
EIGHTEEN

The haze was beginning to lift from Samantha's brain. The growing rage she felt toward Mississippi served to fuel her recovery. Still the question of what she should do next remained. Crockett's offer of safe passage out of Saquarra seemed in many ways to be her only hope. Kane had made no such offer, despite her direct and indirect queries.

Gunshots, in a sudden, combined roar, erupted from the far side of the street. Samantha lowered herself to the floor, feeling more and more like a sitting duck in the close confines of the jail. Overhead she heard two solid thumps against the wooden roof — El Diablo signaling the others below. Her eyes followed Clive Brown, then Kane, marveling at the way the man El Diablo had called El Lobo deliberately squeezed off his shots, one at a time. His face was fixed in a perpetual grimace. He studied the situation very closely each time before squeezing the trigger. Samantha continued to appraise him. Although he wasn't the type to back down, she was certain his chances of succeeding were slim. Crockett's men were far too numerous and more than experienced in taking care of themselves. And there were the others, the temporary residents of

Saquarra, the same breed as those on Crockett's payroll. They would be willing to lend a hand to free the big boss and rid Saquarra of a meddling tin-pan man, an aging sheriff, and a turncoat outlaw who, only a short time earlier, had been one of them. Once Mississippi rallied the troops, they would have no chance at all. Yet, did she have a chance without these three?

A bullet slammed through the office, exploding the oil lamp's chimney in a spectacular shower of splintering glass. A second bullet smacked into the sheriff's bulletin board, hanging on the wall, and a third ricocheted off the bars with a sharp, metallic singing that jerked Kane's head around in her direction.

"You okay?"

She watched Kane's mouth form words but could not discern what he was saying. The noise from the bullets buzzing around the jail echoed in her head.

Over his shoulder Kane called out again: "Samantha, are you all right?"

"Yes . . . yes," she answered, once she could make out his words. Yet all she could think was that in a short time they all would be dead. "Yes," she repeated as the familiar wave of defeat rolled over her.

Another bullet made its way into the jail, hitting the back wall of Samantha's cell. She had to get out of here. The only person who wanted out of the jail as much as she did was Crockett. The volume of the gunfire seemed to be rising in a crescendo. There was no hope for the occupants of the jail — no hope. She remembered the war — that other time when the sound of gunfire was never-ending. Even through her dreams she had heard the constant barrage of bullets. Whether they were real or not didn't matter. She had heard them day and night, night and day, for months on end. Now how many days would the current fighting go on?

She watched Crockett, sitting calmly on the edge of his cot, seemingly not the least bit disturbed by the occasional bullet that found its way inside the jail. She hated him for that. He sat there with a look on his face no different than the one he wore while playing solitaire into the wee hours of the morning in the saloon. Just as neat and unruffled now as he was in the saloon. Samantha hated him for his calm.

Gunfire outside the jail continued to roar like a wave crashing upon the shore, shots following one after the other in such rapid succession that it was difficult to separate them. Samantha's head felt as though it would burst with the noise.

"*Compadres,*" El Diablo called down from his roof-top perch, "I think there are only two."

Two? Samantha blanched at the thought. Only two! How could two men cause so much noise? What would happen if all of Crockett's men decided to storm the jail? She shivered, more determined than ever to get escape.

Kane pulled back from the window. A bullet slammed off the frame, yet he didn't even blink.

"You reckon they're testing us? Looking for a weak spot?" Brown asked Kane.

"No, I think a couple of them are stupid."

Clive chuckled. "Might be, but keep a sharp eye. Stupid men can kill you just as dead as smart ones."

The gunshots continued from outside. They were pounding the jail haphazardly but steadily.

Kane laughed softly, then with practiced ease he returned their fire. The sheriff followed suit. Above, El Diablo's rifle coughed out deliberately paced shots, tracing the outlaws' paths as they parted company, each coming up tight against a side of the jail building.

Kane closed the heavy wooden shutter, listening for any noise that would telegraph their intent. Overhead, there was the occasional shifting of El Diablo's position on the roof. His erratic movements above and the silence of the outlaws' rifles testified to the fact that he, too, had lost track of the attackers' movements. There was no sign of Pike, nothing of his mark in this, making it plain that this was not the main body of the liberating army with which Moody had threatened them.

Easing the shutter open again, Kane drew a shot. Instantly he returned it. El Diablo's rifle cracked sharply at the same instant. It was impossible to tell which slug took the outlaw, but one of the pair outside jerked, threw his hands wide, his weapon flying off into the shadows, and dropped like lead into the dirt.

For a frozen instant the street outside was quiet. Samantha could see the tension in Kane by the set of his shoulders. Then the firing was renewed from outside again, though now the peppering came from only one gun.

"Where the hell is he?" the sheriff demanded. "I can't see a damn' thing around corners!"

212

The bullets, whining in their direction, were gaining accuracy, and the jail, while built like a fort, had too many blind corners to spot the lone attacker from the inside. The roof was a different matter. El Diablo sighted the place between the wagon and the wall in the narrow alley where the dark, lanky man was holed up. He could not get a clear path to the outlaw, but he continued to make him nervous with well-placed bullets.

Then it all changed abruptly. A barrage of lead came at the jail, shots fired in rapid succession by a man fanning his gun. Another stray found its way inside, slamming into the desk and shaving off a huge splinter that sliced across the room and landed only inches from Samantha. Kane threw open his shutter and squeezed off a shot, the report ricocheting around the room.

"That's enough," Samantha whispered to herself. She couldn't stand the noise any longer, and she scuttled in a straight line to the sheriff's desk. She eased open the drawer and grabbed the keys from where she had seen the sheriff put them. She was about to close the drawer when she saw the gun. Slowly she reached out her hand, the cold of the steel providing a second's relief from the heat. Gun in hand, she carefully pushed the drawer back into a closed position. She glanced toward Kane and the sheriff. Neither was looking her way. Her look was then cast in Crockett's direction. The big man was watching her closely, his eyes beaming. Remaining in a squatting position, she slowly swiveled herself around, intent upon making a hasty return to her cell. As she crept toward the safety of her cot, the toe of her shoe caught in the hem of her skirt, and she stumbled. In an effort to upright herself, she dropped the gun and accidentally kicked it, sending it across the distance where it landed directly outside Crockett's cell. Before Samantha could try to recover it, Crockett had already retrieved the gun and returned to his cot.

"Don't say a word," Crockett commanded once Samantha was back in her cell.

Dammit, dammit! was all that went through her head as a deadly calm settled over the jail. The quiet sent a chill up her back despite the fact that sweat was breaking out everywhere on her skin. The smell of gunpowder was strong, and a faint blue haze colored the air. It made Samantha nauseous as did the fact that she had actually contemplated trusting Crockett enough to set him free. She buried her head in her arms, cursing her stupidity.

Across the room Kane closed his shutter with a solid thud. "I think I got him," he stated flatly and slid the stout crossbar in place while the sheriff did the same to the window at which he was stationed. Automatically they both started reloading. The sheriff was the first to break the eerie silence that ensued.

"That takes care of two of them. What next?"

Kane shrugged. "That's up to them."

He glanced toward the cell that housed Samantha and then turned to the sheriff. "Things should be quiet for a spell, I think. I'm going out there and see what's going on, and I might even try to make it to my wagon to get a few things."

Brown looked doubtful. "They'll be layin' for you out there."

"I don't think so. They won't be expectin' anyone to slip outside. But I'd be obliged if you let El Diablo know in case I need cover."

Brown nodded.

Kane slipped out the back door. The moment the door closed behind him, the jailhouse seemed desolate without his presence. Brown moved to the nearest window, unbarred it, and peered out through a narrow crack. Nothing was moving. After a moment he closed the window and moved over to the desk. He climbed up and relayed Kane's message to El Diablo. Then he moved solicitously closer to the open cell where Samantha sat on the edge of the thin, lumpy bunk, her head cradled in her hands.

"You okay, Miss Cameron?"

"Yes, I'm okay, Sheriff," she answered wearily, afraid to look him in the eyes.

Brown cleared his throat before speaking again, pained by the emotional agony he saw etched across her swollen face. "Reckon I could push the desk over closer so's it'd offer some cover next time the shootin' starts."

Samantha made an effort to smile. "Don't bother." She felt a need to keep him close to her. "Why'd you stay on here as sheriff? Why'd you ever want to be one in the first place?"

Brown scratched his jaw. "Those are mighty big questions to answer," he said. "It'd likely take a long spell to give you the story proper."

"Go ahead," Samantha encouraged, "I'm not going anywhere, are you?" Her eyes shifted in Crockett's direction. "Or how about you, Crockett?"

Crockett stared back threateningly. He weighed the options open to him. If he tried to escape now, he would have to kill the sheriff. He didn't want that hanging over his head once he regained power in the town. His only quarry was Pike. For that killing he could command the respect of the people of Saquarra. No, it was better to wait until another attack was underway to make his escape. Still, Samantha's impertinence galled him.

"Welllll . . . ," Brown's long drawn-out word broke the silence and drew the attention of the jail's two occupants, "the idea first came to me when I was ten, I guess. My daddy was coming home one summer day, bringing supplies. I recall it was a scorcher, and it hadn't rained in two months. About two miles from home he was shot. Don't know why, and we never did find out. He didn't die, but he never walked again. I watched him sit in a chair, staring at the walls for the next eight years. He never said a word. It near killed my mother. It just never set right with me that somebody could do that and get away with it. Still don't set right . . ."

CHAPTER
NINETEEN

The town was quiet when Kane slipped out the back door of the jail. Crouching close to the walls, he proceeded from building to building, six-gun clenched in his fist, nerves taut as jerked leather. Saquarra's citizens were obviously making themselves scarce, and Crockett's men were busy over at the saloon where the only commotion in town could be heard. The temptation was strong in Kane to try to eavesdrop so that he could learn their plans, but he knew it to be too risky. Besides, it was going to take them a while to liquor themselves up to the point of action. The wiser move would be to find some of the locals and have a little talk with them.

Reluctantly he pressed on, working his way up the street. In the shade of the building that housed the telegraph he stopped a few feet away from the back door, waiting and listening. Kane tested the door, found it unlocked, and slipped inside, unnoticed as a shadow.

The place was empty. Kane made his way to the front of the office. He doffed his hat and, crouching low, raised his head only enough to bring his eyes to window level to view the main street. He was able to see into many passageways not visible from the limited angle of the jail and found nothing there disturbing. There was no massing of Crockett's troops, no single sharpshooters visible on roof tops. It was as he had figured. For the moment the only activity could be found at the saloon. Once night fell he knew it would be a different story.

Kane vacated the telegraph office, carried by long, effortless strides. He was skirting the edge of Mex-town, circling back toward his wagon for supplies, when he sensed a presence. Aniceta Esquivel appeared as if out of the air.

"*¡Aiii! señor,* you should not be here!" Her voice was kept very low, but her tone was strident.

"I could say the same to you."

She frowned. "Do not make jokes! They will kill you on sight, and there are still many of them in Saquarra to do so."

"Someone had to see what was happening, and I need supplies from my wagon. We might be in that jail quite a spell. The streets are quiet."

"It is not so quiet as it appears. We want to help you. Tell me what it is you need us to do, and we will do it."

"Stay out of the way of the bullets."

"We will do more than that!"

"I don't want you getting yourselves killed."

"This is our war, too," Aniceta said firmly. "We do not wish for any of ours to be killed, but an end must be brought to Crockett's reign. We understand the risk involved. Already there has been trouble at the *cantina.*

Two of ours were wounded trying to escape men Pike sent. Tell me what you wish us to do."

Despite the shelter of the narrow alleyway Kane felt exposed. Old instincts, newly awakened, tingled a warning across the surface of his skin. His mind was working at a furious speed. He had touched a match to the dynamite that was Saquarra, but in one matter Aniceta was correct. It was their fight, too.

"Listen to me, Aniceta. The jail is built like a fort. When the fighting starts, it's going to be close and nasty. We don't want to have to worry about hitting the wrong people. The fewer of you nearby, the better. Tell your people to stay away from the jail. Tell them to take no chances. They must hide, attack, and run. Do small things to trip up the enemy. Ambush those that are alone and only when your people are many. Set up some trip wires around the town. If one of your men is a very good shot, put him on a roof top with good cover. Then move swiftly and do something else. Keep your people scattered and keep them moving."

Aniceta grinned broadly, her round countenance appearing merry in the face of possible death. "It is a good plan. There are those from over the line who will help, too."

"Just keep them away from the jail. Some of the things I intend to do will not discriminate between friend and enemy. You can't be within range. I have enough to worry about with Samantha in the jail."

"I will tell them. Samantha, she is in the jail?"

"I'm trying to protect her from Pike and maybe from herself. That lady's been through a lot."

219

"Perhaps we could smuggle her out of there and take her to our part of the town."

"It's too risky. At this point I think Pike would kill her if he found her . . . along with anyone who helped her. She should be checked by a doctor."

Aniceta pondered that for a moment. "The doctor in Saquarra is gone as usual, and our *curandera* is busy with the wounded who escaped the *cantina*. But, if you come with me, perhaps she can give you something that will help."

He followed her deeper into the deadline. The healer Aniceta spoke of was only a couple of doors away. They entered the small house through a side door opening on the alley between high false-fronted buildings. The *curandera*, a blocky, middle-aged woman with coal-black hair and a stern but kindly face, hurried to them, clasping Aniceta's extended hand in both of hers. She spoke no English, but, when Aniceta told her of Samantha, she hurried off. She returned with two small pouches of herbs. The contents of one was to drink to stop internal bleeding, if there was any; the other contained items that would cleanse and soothe her external injuries. Aniceta also handed Kane a bundle of food to take back to the jail.

These are good people, Kane thought to himself. "Remember to tell everyone what I have said," he reminded her as he readied himself to leave. "Warn them of the dangers and . . . good luck."

As he slipped away, Aniceta whispered: "We will be there, *Señor* Kane. *Vaya con Dios.*"

220

In the fading gray light of dusk, Mississippi Pike directed his men to their positions for the assault on the jail. He had stationed two men at the hotel to wait until it was dark at which time they were to make their ascent to the roof. Thus far they appeared to be following orders as they had not drawn any fire from the jail, unlike the hapless pair who had earlier launched their own assault, and for this Pike was congratulating himself on his generalship. The men with him saw his plan as one designed to free Crockett and regain control of Saquarra. As far as Pike was concerned, they still controlled the town. After all, hadn't the Mexs scattered like prairie rats when his men hit the *cantina?* It was his intention now to rid himself of Crockett and his captors in the jail. The big man's end was at hand, and it was going to be easier than first anticipated.

Most of the townspeople had fled, hiding somewhere. He had managed to keep a wary eye on Harlan Moody, the bartender, positioning the man as look-out. He knew Moody was afraid of him, and, when he had issued the order to Moody, there had been no balking. The livery owner, Ben Ford, had disappeared, and Red Grissom was nowhere to be found. Pike decided they had probably slipped off to a rat hole somewhere to wait this thing out. None of the good folks was anywhere to be seen. It was time to stand up and be counted, and they were invisible. In fact, the whole town was quiet. Few lights showed as the sun dipped down behind the western mountains.

Pike remained in the shadows as his men moved into position around the jail. From where he was stationed, he could see most of the town and keep an eye on the roof of the jail where he knew that damn' Mex outlaw kept watch. He enjoyed his position of power, watching everything settle into place. This fight would prove his ability as undisputed leader. That Crockett would not come out of it alive was the thing on which Pike must concentrate his efforts. He was confident it would be an easy victory.

Kane and his cohorts had managed a daring raid earlier that morning, and they had done him a service in removing Crockett. Now the tables would be turned. He would have the advantage of surprise, and there was nowhere for them to run. Once the torch was put to the jail, it would go up like cottonwood. Those inside would be forced to abandon their only refuge. When they came running out, picking them off would be easy. He just wanted to be stationed where he could get a clear shot at Crockett. And then there was Samantha.

Rubbing his left arm and shoulder where the pieces of buckshot had caught him that morning, he winced, swearing softly. He eyes were on the jail and could see a tiny flicker of light filtering through a crack in one of the heavy shutters that locked the place up tighter than a fort. Idly Pike glanced around the town. A light now showed here and there, though all of them shone through tightly drawn curtains or heavy storm shutters. They were cowed all right; his grip was solid. Things would fall into line once this was settled. He smiled faintly and resumed his observation of the jail.

Kane, having returned to the jailhouse, had joined El Diablo on the roof top. Occasionally one of them would catch the suggestion of movement or a sound below, but they could detect nothing certain enough for a clear shot, so they held their fire, knowing cartridges might become precious later.

The peddler handed El Diablo a chunk of dried-out cheese, some hard tack, and a stretch of jerky. "Don't want your stomach rumblin', giving us away up here."

"Do not worry, *amigo mio*. My stomach ees well trained. It has gone empty many times for days. What could it do? I had nothing to give it."

"Eat."

El Diablo shrugged and took a bite. "You are a grand fool to risk your neck for this." He tore off a large chunk of the jerky with his teeth and nodded toward the street below. "It will be soon, I think."

Kane nodded his agreement. He had always been able to see well in the dark, like an owl, but this was a moonless night, and even such a bird would have difficulty spotting its prey on a night like this. He found himself restless, eager for the deadly dance to resume.

His edginess telegraphed itself to El Diablo, and the outlaw recognized the reason for it. The woman below.

"You do not trust this Cameron woman, eh, El Lobo?" El Diablo asked flatly. His gaze left Kane and moved to the street below.

Kane looked El Diablo's way. "No, dammit," he answered evenly, "I don't."

"You expect her to betray us?"

"If she thought she was helping . . . I saw Crockett talking to her . . . God knows what he was promising her." He paused for several seconds. "And I think she's afraid that we all might die here . . . that she's on the losing side."

El Diablo chuckled. "She ees wrong, *mi compadre.* Have you not told her so?"

"I tried," Kane shrugged, "but she was too scared to pay much attention."

"Too bad . . ." El Diablo's words were cut off as gunfire erupted on all sides of them like the onslaught of a sudden storm.

Wood cracked and splintered around them as bullets screamed up from below. The wolf and the devil found themselves with plenty of cover. They maneuvered for a position from which they could most advantageously return the fire. Once in place the muzzle flashes of weapons guided their aim.

"Save it till you have a clear target," Kane said loudly enough to be heard above the gunfire.

He grabbed the special shotgun he had brought up with him, leaned against the roof's upright support, shielding himself from the hail of bullets, and squeezed the trigger. A load of nails exploded in a starburst pattern driven by a big load of gunpowder.

Someone screamed down on the street, and El Diablo chuckled his satisfaction. "*¡Aiii!* I would never have thought of that!"

"A man had to make do with what he had during the war," Kane said bitterly as the barrage of gunfire lessened, fading to a few sporadic shots.

"Maybe so, but not all are so inventive."

"I'm gonna let 'em get settled so they can ponder this shotgun's payload. Then, as you would say, El Diablo, 'El Lobo will prowl.'"

El Diablo laughed, and then looked quizzically at Kane. *"Por favor?"*

"I'll slip out of the jail and go after them one at a time." He put down the shotgun and picked up the rifle once again.

With his swarthy coloring El Diablo showed himself above the high, protective wall of the jail, dark against dark, almost invisible against the night sky. He drew the wild shot he sought, lead whizzing past him, going wide, proving to his assailant that he was less than sure of his target. With the muzzle flash from below to guide him, El Diablo was sure. His response was swift, and the resulting yowl from below was a satisfying sound. Instantly he dropped to cover. Bullets snapped through the air above him like a swarm of angry bees. He sprawled for a moment, laughing, while Kane pressed tightly against the wall for protection against the sudden return of hot lead.

El Diablo had a deadly eye and moved like a phantom, a peculiar half smile twisting his lips. "My fren'," he shouted, "we both are very foolish, very brave, or very crazy."

"Maybe . . . ," Kane responded as he shifted his position yet again, "we are all three."

"Perhaps I will accompany you on your rounds."

"I would like it better if you stayed here."

"I do not like being closed in, *amigo mio*."

"I could have guessed as much, considering how you acted below in the jail. But out here you have a canopy of stars overhead. The air is fresh and clear. You can barely smell the gunpowder. What better place than this?"

El Diablo chuckled, but it was nervous and dry. The cool kiss of the night air on his skin gave welcome respite, yet the instinct to prowl was as strong in him as it was in El Lobo. He did not know what drove the wolf, but for himself it was an extension of his abhorrence of closed-in spaces.

The firing quieted, and a thick silence settled over the street. El Diablo cut loose with a blood-curdling yell. Kane grinned, wondering what the men in the street below made of the shrieking wail that sounded like it came from a demented man.

Some fool showed himself, and El Diablo fired. A volley of shots followed in return, but El Diablo folded to the roof, already out of range. He shifted to another position by rolling across the roof.

Below the sheriff yelled up: "Christ, what the hell was that!"

"The devil and the wolf," was the response along with a chuckle from El Diablo above.

Below, several more bullets thudded against the exterior of the jail. Sheriff Brown threw open the shutter to return fire just as several more came slamming into the room.

Samantha cringed from her position on the floor, her fingers wrapped in a cramped knot around the tin cup of foul-tasting brew the sheriff had given her. Since

Kane's return to the jail with a host of supplies, including the herbs from which her beverage was concocted, she had avoided looking at Crockett. She was tense, waiting for him to make his move.

More gunshots. They came so quickly the ear-splitting sounds rolled together in an indistinguishable pounding. The bitter herbal brew now soured on her tongue. Samantha trembled, the liquid sloshing violently in the cup. Unconsciously she clenched the keys she kept wrapped in the folds of her skirt with a strength that drove them deep into the skin of her hand.

Saquarra's head man was not distracted by the gunfire. With all the commotion there would be no better time to make his escape.

"Samantha," Crockett whispered harshly, his voice low, nearly inaudible above the continual pounding of gunfire. "Samantha, give me the keys, *now*."

Samantha wanted to ignore him but was drawn to look anyway. She swallowed deeply as she realized the full impact of what she was being asked to do. "I can't do that to . . . these people," she stumbled over her words, knowing Crockett would laugh at her newly found sense of loyalty.

"Give me the keys, Samantha, or I'll shoot your sheriff friend in the back," Crockett whispered as he brought the gun out from its hiding place and leveled it in Brown's direction.

"I can't," she stammered.

He cocked the gun. "I'm not playing games, Samantha. I'll do it."

She glanced in Brown's direction. He was preoccupied fully with the activity outside. His back made a perfect target. Samantha knew, as Crockett did, that there would be no better time to make an escape. With Kane and El Diablo on the roof, the sheriff had his hands full. But God, what was she doing? Crockett was just another version of Pike, maybe even worse.

"Samantha, the keys."

She had no choice. Slowly she slid the keys between the bars along the floor into Crockett's waiting hands.

Unexpectedly there was a pause in the shooting punctuated by a banshee scream from overhead. Sheriff Brown slammed the heavy shutter closed for a moment's reprieve as he reloaded his gun. His eyes touched on Samantha where she sat frozen. Samantha's heart pulsed erratically. Brown's kindly eyes held her, and his face broke into a reassuring smile. Sheriff Brown was a good man, Samantha reflected, something she had never realized until today. But now Crockett had the keys. There was no turning back.

Brown's gun reloaded, he threw open the shutters. His full attention once again was concentrated on the fight outside.

Samantha dropped to the floor unthinkingly. The tin cup clattered along the floorboards, clanking against the cell bars, brown liquid soaking into dry wood. She pulled herself up tightly as the firing continued in sporadic bursts. Icy fear clutched at her as the shooting built toward a crescendo once again. She glanced at Crockett who was watching the sheriff's every move.

228

Crockett crept cautiously but hastily to the cell door. He put the key in the lock. He nudged the door open and slipped out of the cell without mishap. He kept one eye on the sheriff as he moved to the door of Samantha's cell. He swept inside and placed the gun barrel against the side of her head as he jerked her from the floor, warning her to keep her mouth shut.

It all happened so quickly Samantha didn't have time to react before it was too late. Her body now provided a shield as she cried out.

"You're a bigger fool than I thought," Crockett whispered as he leveled the gun in the sheriff's direction. "Don't even think about it, Brown," he warned.

CHAPTER
TWENTY

The Mexican named Miguel carried an old Enfield rifle he had gotten off some raiding Indians a couple of years back. Swiftly he moved up the darkened main street of Mex-town, his young wife, Maria, close behind him. The gun was loaded, but, since the weapon was a single-shot cap and ball model, he would get only one chance to use it effectively. He was prepared for that event.

"We must pick a good spot," Maria whispered urgently, hurrying along in his wake, carrying the small pouches of black powder, lead balls, and percussion caps.

"Do not worry, Maria."

"And we will not stay long."

"No. I will fire the rifle, and we will be gone like rabbits down the hole."

"Good. Because I am very afraid."

"Me too, *querida,* but we all must do what we can to help the peddler."

With darkness as their cloak they slipped across the line, eluding a couple of Pike's men. Miguel led the way up the saloon's back steps. He had not been telling Maria any falsehoods to comfort her. He was afraid.

Pike's men were overconfident, but they were numerous and scattered everywhere throughout Saquarra. One false step could be the end of them both. Yet, he was more afraid to leave Maria alone. His wish was that it would be his good fortune to end the life of that dog, Mississippi Pike.

"We will go to *Señor* Ford's stable after I make the shot," Miguel told Maria as they made their way to the saloon roof, watching for Crockett's men with every step. "We'll be able to reload there and then find another target."

Once they attained the roof, they settled back for a few moments, Miguel casting his eyes up and down the shadowy street, finger curled lightly about the trigger. He could see a small knot of men on the hotel roof and was thankful he had not chosen it as his first vantage point. The thought of just such a misstep brought renewed sweat to his brow. The night's darkness made choosing a target difficult. Then suddenly Miguel's wish was answered. In a spill of lamplight Mississippi Pike stood near the gun shop, well out of range from the top of the jail, but not out of his range. Miguel smiled nervously. He lined up his shot and hesitated that extra moment. This was what he had wanted, but killing a man from ambush did not sit well with Miguel. His finger was taking up the slack on the trigger when Maria touched his shoulder.

"Look!"

He jerked his attention from Pike, heeding the urgency in his wife's tone, and looked toward the hotel roof where she was pointing.

Torches had been lit and a growing pool of light spread over their heads as more flared to life. Several men had worked their way to the edge of the roof nearest the jail, and their intent was plain. They were going to try to send those torches over to the jail and burn them out.

Miguel gasped. He shifted his rifle and took fresh aim. He had but one shot, and he made it pay. His weapon's booming roar thundered across Saquarra, and the man nearest the roof's edge suddenly jerked and sprawled, torch spilling from his hand to the roof. An instant later flames were shimmering across the roof's tinder-dry wood. Heads turned in the direction of the shot. Miguel cursed, grabbed Maria by the arm, and they dashed for the edge of the saloon roof, seeking shelter from possible gunfire directed at them from the hotel. They were over the edge and scurrying into the darkness before the first shot sounded. Elsewhere in Saquarra voices, sharp and strident, sounded, and a dull roar vibrated the air.

Below at the jail Samantha, wincing with pain, held her side and moved quickly along with Crockett who still used her as a shield as they ducked out the back door. They stepped free of the jail at the same moment the blast from Miguel's gun took down the man on the hotel roof. Samantha went rigid. The sound was terrifying. Then she was being dragged forcefully along.

Kane spotted the torches as they leapt to life on the hotel roof.

"Crazy fool. He's going to try to burn us out."

232

"Not so crazy," El Diablo returned. "It will work. Once the flames catch we cannot stay here."

Kane cursed Pike for the dangerous idiot he was. El Diablo was right, but it was a helluva lot worse than that. If the fire caught, not only would the jail burn down, but the entire town with it. There was no telling when the last rain had fallen. The wood of the town buildings had been baking and drying out in the sun for months. It would be like dropping a match in a hay loft.

"Don't let them throw those things!" Kane said urgently just as Miguel's Enfield roared, and the front man of the torch-bearing pack sprawled on the roof, releasing his firebrand. The catastrophe was almost instantaneous. Those gathered on the hotel roof scattered and leaped about to snuff out the flames.

Across the way Kane shifted his aim to the hotel roof and started firing with a steady rhythm. El Diablo rose on one knee, an apparition from hell, lips twisted in a murderous sneer, and also opened fire.

"*Aie yi yi!*" he called to Kane above the chatter of gunfire as the flames danced and swayed on torches held aloft, snapping upward into the dry air. "I had not thought of that."

"Crossed my mind," Kane admitted, "but I never figured Pike to be such a god damned fool. I didn't think he would be willing to destroy the prize he wants. The whole damn' town is wood!"

Abruptly a flaming torch was hefted out from the hotel roof, descending toward them in a blazing spiral. Almost instantly it was followed by a second, and a third, lighting up the night sky like falling stars. Before the first one even hit, El Diablo was moving, snatching off his worn jacket, beating at the flames as smoldering wood bounced with a spray of sparks to the roof top. A second and third dropped, while he worked, igniting the dry wood. Fingers of flame crackled and spread in myriad directions, defying him as he pounded at them like a madman. Then, dropping to one knee, he fired repeatedly. Several men fell, either wounded or dead, but more torches followed, propelled by howls of fury from the opposite roof.

Kane stepped out into the open, centering his gun between two of the upraised torches, and fired. The twin torches flipped backwards, and the flames were suddenly gathering and coalescing on the hotel roof, spreading quickly in a rising breeze. Startled, angry yells continued to rise along with the thickening smoke. For the moment Kane's action drew the attention from the jail roof top to that of the hotel.

"Fire!" the clarion call rang from the darkened street below. "We've got fire!"

Probably there were few more dreaded words in the West — or any other place where men congregated. And in Saquarra the cry of fire was even more of a nightmare. Wood, once intended to shore up the mines, was long dried beneath sun and wind. Unless something were done quickly the whole of Saquarra would soon be an inferno.

The fire spread on the wings of rising wind, climbing down the extended front of the jail and spreading along the sides toward the boardwalk. Unbridled, the flames leapt high into the air, the intense heat finally driving back any attempt to smother them. Smoke billowed up in huge, almost white clouds, snatching the moisture from their nostrils and filling their lungs, though Kane and El Diablo still made vain, abortive attempts to smother the fire around them.

Gunfire had died to nothing because any kind of target had become invisible in the smoke-filled air. The peddler and the outlaw were lost from sight in undulating waves of smoke that billowed skyward from the jail's roof. Pike's men had already abandoned the hotel which was becoming engulfed in flames. Sweat ran in rivers on both El Diablo and Kane in response to the rising heat.

Kane walked to the center of the roof, where he was joined by El Diablo, and lifted the trap door. "We can't fight it," Kane shouted above the roar of the flames. "We have to get out of here . . . down and out the back."

"I can't go down there," El Diablo protested.

"No choice. You'll be roasted up here."

"I will go over the side."

"They'll nail you before you can think to let go and drop to the ground."

"My choice, my risk, *amigo mio.*"

Kane looked down and shook his head. Then, without warning, he grabbed El Diablo by the shoulder. "I'm afraid not!" he shouted above the fury as he shoved El Diablo through the trap door before him.

Small sections of the roof were ready to collapse as Kane flung himself in the outlaw's wake. It would not be long before the roof caved in.

Sheriff Brown was grim, his attention divided between concern over what might happen to Samantha and the shooting from outside. When Crockett had made his break, he had not been able to get a certain shot at him because of his use of Samantha as a shield. Now his voice was hoarse from yelling to get the attention of Kane or El Diablo to let them know what had happened. He understood — the sounds of the fire overhead and the smoke curling down in gathering clouds against the ceiling told him all he needed to know. Yet he did not want to risk leaving his station to go up to the roof. So, whenever there was a lull in the confusion, he let out a holler.

Finally he could hear talking above. The trap door was thrown open. Before he could say anything, El Diablo rained down from above, landing clumsily on the desk, and then pitching over the side.

He was followed by Kane's more graceful entry.

"Crockett's gone!" Brown shouted. "He took Samantha."

"When? How'd it happen?" Kane wanted to know.

"Not more then ten minutes ago. I had my hands full down here . . . I don't know how he got the keys. I tried to call up to you, but then all hell broke loose. Are they crazy with this fire idea?"

"We've got to find her, and we will, if she's out there. Now, out the back way!" Kane yelled, snatching up what supplies he could lay his hands on, gratified to see the sheriff do the same.

El Diablo remained frozen, leaning against the desk, sweat spilling down from his face, eyes fixed on the descending smoke.

"Move!" Kane yelled in his face.

There was no response.

"What the hell?" The sheriff was looking into El Diablo's face which was set in a rictus of fear so profound it shook the lawman to his heels. Neither knew that El Diablo's biggest fear as a child locked in the closet had been one of fire.

The creaking, groaning wood being consumed by the flames convinced Kane there was no more time to spare. He dug his fingers into El Diablo's shoulders and, with the effort it took to uproot a small tree, wrenched him free, propelling him brutally toward the door.

Kane continued to push El Diablo; the sheriff, without thought, pulled. They stumbled to the back, bombarded by falling, sparking débris. Kane flung the door open wide, sucking a gale-force wind howling in through the door, drawing the smoke downward in a choking cloud.

"Get out! Now!"

He maneuvered El Diablo before him, gave a mighty push, and followed behind with the sheriff. They stopped in the shadows just outside the orange light cast by the flames, spreading and leaping overhead. Wood popped all around them like combined pistol shots, and a long, drawn-out roar emanated from inside the jail.

CHAPTER
TWENTY-ONE

The outbreak of fires had changed the course of the fight. It had been Crockett's plan, once he escaped from the jail, to rally a few trustworthy men to escort him back to his office from where he would orchestrate the remainder of the battle. He had intended to use Samantha as a lure to draw in Pike for the final showdown. Now all that was changed by the course of events. The streets were filled with combatants and non-combatants alike, all of whose attention was focused on containing the flames at the jail and the hotel before the whole town burned to the ground.

Crockett pulled Samantha into the shadows of the general store where he could observe the goings-on and determine his next move. He watched in amazement as the flames crept down the walls of the hotel. The guests from inside were making hurried exits, their arms filled with their possessions. Those guests who were not occupying their rooms at the time of the outbreak appeared from various directions to gather what belongings they could while there was still time. All the while the hotel owner stood in front of the burning building, looking on without hope.

Frank Crockett then glanced toward the jail. He spotted the trio of Kane, El Diablo, and Brown leaving. It was all he needed to see. He couldn't risk being spotted by the tin-pan man. He had to find a hiding place for himself and Samantha. He tightened his grasp on Samantha's wrist and started for the livery.

They had gone no more than twenty feet when a gun cracked sharply above the rustling roar of the spreading inferno. Crockett jerked in mid-stride, gave one long, audible sigh, and ploughed headlong into the dust, his grasp still tight on Samantha's wrist, dragging her down with him.

Samantha hit the ground on her knees with a jarring force that sent a knife-like pain searing up one leg which doubled her over as a second gunshot split the air above her head. "No!" she screamed. She tried to jerk her wrist from Crockett's grip, but it would not give way. Choked by a rising terror, she beat at the man's lifeless fingers. She wanted to scream again, but a deadly calm descended upon her as one galvanizing thought flashed through her head. *It's Mississippi.* He was the one who fired the shot that killed Crockett, and now he would be after her. *Not if I get him first,* she thought. The words of her mother echoed again through her head: *No one is ever going to help you, Sammy, so you gotta learn to help yourself.* Now methodically she disengaged Crockett's fingers one by one from her wrist. Then she laid flat and began to search the ground for the gun Crockett had been carrying, the gun she had foolishly let slip from her hand in the jail.

When she found it, she crawled into the nearest shadows to check the gun's chambers. She would have four chances to kill Mississippi . . . as he tried to kill her. If she was successful, she would run as far away as possible. Away from Mississippi, away from Kane, and away from Saquarra. She gathered the folds of her skirt in one hand and took off at a limping run.

Kane saw Samantha just as her silhouette disappeared, mixing among the many shadows created by the flames. For the moment he could do nothing as the three of them were pinned behind the jail. Closely spaced, well-placed shots, coming from two directions, precluded any rescue attempt.

The jail's roof was beginning to fold in on itself, and in seconds the flames would undoubtedly reach the supplies he had brought from his wagon. The wall which had provided shelter from hot lead was bowing. They had no choice but to move now. The heat emanating from the blaze was insufferable. Together the trio moved away from the building, Kane guiding El Diablo as he espied the watering trough that would afford cover. Sheriff Brown covered their retreat, his gun spouting bullets. A thunderous blast then shook the ground beneath them and sent the air shimmering in undulating waves.

"¡Santa Maria! What was that?" El Diablo exclaimed, jolted out of his daze.

"Gunpowder," Kane informed him. "Had it in my stores. Thought we might be able to use some extra."

240

Next a spray of colorful sparks danced against the night sky. Both the sheriff and El Diablo gave their companion another quizzical look.

"Fireworks. Might've come in handy," Kane explained further.

Sparks drifted and skittered on the waves of the wind, threatening to touch off new fires where they landed, still smoldering. A section of boardwalk flamed, and a tiny rivulet of fire inched along like a river. A section of fence burned up against the livery wall, sending out a tendril to test the weathered wood.

El Diablo breathed deeply of the fresh air. Muscles that had been held taut and rigid back in the jail were unwinding with a burning pain. His unclenched jaw now ached, and his eyes gritted in their sockets.

"You all right?" Kane asked him.

El Diablo shuddered. He had openly revealed his greatest weakness. He cast wary eyes between the peddler and the sheriff.

"Sí, gracias." He owed these men who had saved his life an explanation. His pride was not important among friends. Besides, he could not allow them to believe he had merely panicked. "It was the closed-in space. It is a fear from my childhood. No one knows of this weakness." He drew his hand gun, checked it, and looked meaningfully from one to the other.

"No one else ever will," Kane assured him.

Sheriff Brown added a curt nod of compliance. "Sure ain't gonna have that problem in this town again any time soon by the time the fire gets done with it anyway," he added, eyes scanning the blaze.

More buildings were catching fire, fanned by the increasing winds. Gunshots continued to pop, crack, and roar on all sides, ringing and thudding above the continual roar of the wild fire.

Kane was readying himself to go after Samantha when citizens of Saquarra began appearing. At first there were just a few, then a few more, and soon it seemed everyone from both sides of the deadline was filling up the streets. Some waved guns or other objects they had picked up which they could use as a weapon. Others started a bucket line from the well out behind the livery and another from behind the hotel, though none was kidding himself into believing he could save any of the structures.

"We need a plan, Kane," he heard from more than one.

As Samantha ran from shadow to shadow, she dodged the sailing sparks and pieces of flaming débris. Her only thought was to find Mississippi. As she ran past the gun shop, a new thought formed in her mind.

The back door was open, and Samantha ducked inside. One corner of the north wall had ignited, and a trickle of flames inched along the floor in that area. She criss-crossed the floor and slipped behind the counter, scanning the boxes of ammunition. She snatched up a box of bullets when she found the right ones.

The trail of fire danced across the wooden floor and caught the hem of her skirt as she turned away to make her retreat. She slapped the flame out, which left a dark, smoldering spot in her skirt. As she scrubbed at the skirt to make sure it was no longer burning, she lost precious time. It was then she heard voices.

"Let's get all the guns and ammunition out before it's too late."

Samantha turned toward the back door but saw that way was blocked by the spreading fire. She whirled back into the room, searching frantically for an avenue of escape. As she tried to see beyond the billowing smoke, she clutched the box of shells to her chest like a talisman, unwilling to give it up.

The voices were gaining in volume, nearing the door. She would have to chance it. She rushed past the three men as they entered the shop.

"What the hell?" one questioned as she brushed past.

Outside the roar was maddening. There was little doubt that the attempts to quell the flames were useless.

Samantha raced down the back alley toward the saloon, determined to find Mississippi. Gun now fully loaded, she carried the extra shells in her skirt pocket, having abandoned the cumbersome box in favor of holding her skirts clear of her feet with her free hand. She was breathless, and the smoke stung eyes already swollen from Pike's beating. Suddenly she felt her foot catch on something, and she took a headlong dive into the dust. It was only by the grace of God that the gun she carried did not go off, though the pain she felt at impact did not make her think much of God's good grace. Placing her hands flat on the ground to push herself back up, she felt several sharp pokes in her back and eased herself back down to avoid the painful pressure. She turned her head around and saw a man's wielding a pitchfork. She gasped, and the man drew back.

"*¡Aiiii!* By all the saints! You could have been dead!" The thick Mexican accent made Samantha cringe. Then she realized he had not meant to hurt her and elbowed her way backward, away from the sharp-pronged implement.

"Get away from here, *señorita! Pronto!*"

Samantha was barely to her feet when Roary Sikes appeared out of the darkness less than ten feet away, gun drawn.

"Got some kinda tricks hid here, greaser?" Sikes sneered. "You and yer pals having a good time?"

The small, wiry, black-haired man positioned himself between Samantha and Sikes. "Go," he repeated over his shoulder to her, "*rapido!*"

Samantha was sure, if she left, her erstwhile defender was as good as dead. At least with the gun she had in her hand they would both have a chance. The light caused by the fire was deceiving, advancing, then retreating. Flickering and casting ghostly shadows, it served to conceal Samantha's jerking movement as she brought the gun up. How was she to make the Mexican retreat from the line of fire?

"You ain't worth spit, you miserable lil' Mex! Get outa my way!" Sikes said as he advanced toward the trembling man.

"What about me?" Samantha interjected as she stepped around and in front of the Mexican. "It's me you really want, isn't it?"

244

Sikes, rattled by her defiant attitude, stood at attention once he saw the gun in her hand. Then a wicked leer turned the corners of his mouth. "You may be right, Miss Cameron, once Pike is dead, you'll be in need of a new protector." He advanced toward her ever so slowly.

Samantha found it difficult to keep her eyes on his face, knowing that in just a few more steps he would be felled by the same wire that had tripped her.

"You're a miserable dog, Sikes, and you don't deserve to live any more than Pike does," Samantha taunted him in an attempt to keep his focus on her.

It worked. Her words emboldened him, and he made a rush for her only to find himself careening forward, a look of surprise his only expression in the flickering, golden light. The Mexican sentry reacted swiftly, swinging his pitchfork upward to catch Sikes on his downward fall. In an instant it was over. Sikes lay dead, his blood soaking into the dust.

"Now, go!" shouted the Mexican. "Do not make me say it again!"

"*Gracias,*" Samantha said as she turned to continue down the alley.

On the main street Kane saw the flames catch and spring up in monstrous form along the front of the livery. His horse was inside, along with almost every other animal worth anything in Saquarra.

"We have to get the horses out of the livery!" he shouted above the roaring crackle of the ever-expanding maëlstrom.

Here and there a gunshot punctuated the disaster that Saquarra had become, a sharp contrast to the thrumming roar of the flames. People ran in all directions, carrying buckets of water or heavy woolen blankets soaked down with which to slap back the flames. Their activities were directed at the buildings in the south end of the town, closer to the deadline. The conflagration was already so wide-spread few took any particular notice of the endangered livery — few except for the livery's owner, Ben Ford. Stout and rumpled, black hair flying in the night wind, he came running from the hotel fire where he had spied the flames leaping to his own business.

"I'm going after the animals," Kane bellowed to his two companions. "We need to find Samantha or Pike. Look for them after you send a bucket brigade over here. I'll join you as soon as we get the horses out of there."

Maria appeared at the back corner of the livery, smoke-smudged and frantic.

"Miguel is in there! My husband! He went after the horses, and he hasn't come out. I'm afraid he is hurt. I cannot reach him. Someone, please, help Miguel!"

Kane was being torn in too many directions. He thought again about Samantha. She was out there somewhere in this holocaust. And so was Pike. But for the moment he was here, and he could not abandon Miguel and the horses.

"We'll have to try to go in from the other side. The fire isn't as bad there yet," Ford shouted.

The peddler was already on his way, feet churning the dust. He slapped his neckerchief in the watering trough along the way, tying it across his nose and mouth on the run. Ford, much to his surprise, was right behind him. In the background he could hear someone shouting directives to those arriving with the water buckets. Several riders, members of Crockett's crowd, pounded past on horses eager to be clear of the disaster. A couple of gunshots cracked nearby.

Kane and Ford made it inside the livery. Ford threw his arms up over his face before the onslaught of heat and smoke, his own neckerchief moistened and tied across his face. He stood next to the tin-pan man, hesitant and waiting for instructions.

"You see him?" Kane barked, eyes streaming tears as the smoke crawled across the earthen floor in the wake of sparks, leaping from wood to bits of straw and back to dry wood, rising in fitful clouds around them.

"No, can't see a damn' thing," Ben snapped back.

"Let's get what horses we can out of here while we look for him."

Equine shrieks and whinnies filled their ears as they ran down the aisle that divided the stalls, throwing open the gates, freeing the terrified animals, and sending them racing toward the livery's north entrance and the promise of fresh air. Ben dragged a yearling to the door as Kane confronted a stubborn, fear-frozen, buckskin dancing among the sparks in his stall. He grabbed a horse blanket off the rails, tossed it over the animal's head, hugging it close beneath his arm, and coaxed the reluctant animal toward the door. When he was nearly at the door, he jerked the blanket free, slapped the buckskin forcefully on the rump, and sent him bolting for freedom.

Then, using the blanket to slap at the floor fires, Kane spotted Miguel. The man lay sprawled in the straw, sparks touching off tiny fires all around him. Kane continued to use the horse blanket to slap out the flames threatening to engulf the smaller man as Ben Ford darted back into the livery.

"Timbers are groaning! We're gonna lose the roof! It's comin' down any second. Come on!"

Kane hoisted Miguel as if he were a sack of grain, tossed him over his shoulder, and, together with Ben, raced through the swirling, spark-filled smoke for the door. A horrible croak, like the sound of a dying giant, set Kane's pulse racing. It was going to be close. In the same instant, with a mighty roar, the livery began collapsing from north to south. Hot air rushed at them in an uncontrolled torrent, sparks diving at them in a stinging eddy. They stumbled through the door frame as it sank to one side, then folded over on its other side.

Both men emerged, coughing and choking. Their lungs convulsed in protest as they were enveloped by their own stale smell of sweat and singed hair. Maria rushed forward, throwing herself with joy at Miguel on the ground were Kane had released his human load. Kane had remained on his knees after letting down Miguel. What he had carried out of that stable had been dead weight. The sound of Maria's wails confirmed his fear. Miguel was beyond help.

248

"I'm so sorry, Maria," he offered by way of solace. "He was in the smoke too long."

All of Saquarra now was filled with the billowing, smothering, smoke. The night sky was tinged a brilliant orange by the flaming town. Several buildings on the north side were not yet in flames, but it was only a matter of time before they would be. Nothing could stop the holocaust Mississippi Pike had unleashed. It was a certainty that the rising sun would shine down on nothing more than smoldering rubble on this side of the deadline. Kane's shoulders slumped from exhaustion as he regained his feet, but his fear for Samantha buoyed him, and he broke into a rhythmic trot.

Where would she have gone? He had to chose between Mex-town and the north end of town as the two most likely places to find her. The north side of town seemed the more logical. With nearly every wooden building in town in flames, it would not be long before nothing remained to take cover behind, save charred wood. And the fight was not over yet. There was Mississippi as well as what remained of Crockett and his forces to consider. How many remained in town, and how many of those were still alive?

Kane edged his way northward. He wiped the back of his hand across eyes which would take some time to recover fully from his trip into the burning livery. Water streamed from them as stinging smoke washed over him in a cloud. Through the blur Kane searched for some sign of Samantha, El Diablo, or Brown. He moved on quickly. *If Pike has already found her . . . ?* He wouldn't allow himself to finish the thought.

Crossing the street in a running half-crouch, he drew a shot from his left side. He could not place its exact source so kept moving, diving headlong for cover between the blazing gun shop and the general store where the fire had finally gained purchase on the roof.

Pinned beside a water trough, Kane waited. He saw Red Grissom, the gunsmith, standing far back from the intense heat, watching helplessly as his gun shop burned. His head dropped to his chest and wagged slowly back and forth like a wounded bull buffalo. Beyond him, people were beginning to pull back, realizing their fight was futile. There were few signs of any of Crockett's men about. That, though, did not mean they were not close at hand.

Elbowing his way along the dusty ground to the other side of the trough, Kane brushed the stinging sweat from his eyes. He lay quietly, barely breathing, ears straining to separate other noises from the all-consuming power of the flames. He squinted against the stinging of the smoke when he caught a flash of Samantha's brown skirt disappear around a corner, headed toward the saloon.

Another gunshot, very near, took a corner out of the wooden trough, and Kane drew back, swearing. An instant later there was another shot, this one the blast of a heavy shotgun, a familiar sound. A startled cry was cut short, and the peddler raised his head to peak around the corner of the trough. He jumped to his knees, cursing, when he encountered the grinning face of El Diablo staring back at him.

CHAPTER
TWENTY-TWO

The outlaw chuckled at Kane's startled and angry reaction. Kane eased the hammer of his gun back down. A bloody cut ran along the side of El Diablo's neck, and flecks of blood spattered his shirt from shoulder to wrist. In addition, a slowly spreading stain soaked the entire left side of his shirt, working its way toward his belt.

"You're hurt!" Kane stated.

"No more than a nick," El Diablo said, dismissing the injury with nothing but a shrug.

"Me . . . well, just got a bit singed," Brown added to the conversation as he squatted down next to El Diablo. "We got lots a dead bodies, but no sign of Pike. Folks are gatherin' on the south end of town, near the deadline, takin' the wounded there. Crockett's down, and most of his boys rode out before the livery went. The good folks of Saquarra come up with an army and fought a mighty impressive war. Scared a lot of them bandits off and even some of Crockett's men. Sure caused a lot of damage after not doing anything about this for months now." He gave Kane a tired smile. "Looks like we've won. Now it's just a matter of stopping Pike . . . and finding Samantha. I haven't had any luck."

Brown's voice had the ring of more than a concerned sheriff. His attitude toward Samantha, since she had been brought to the jail, had warmed considerably.

"I just saw her a minute ago in the alley, but some bullets distracted me," Kane said, slapping his hands against his thighs as he surveyed the street around him. "We'll spread out. If either of you finds Pike, don't spare the bullets, though I'd personally like to tear him apart."

The outlaw and the sheriff headed up Saquarra's main thoroughfare, each drifting to opposite sides of the street. El Diablo swung around to the front of the sputtering remains of the gun shop, while Brown trotted off farther down the line of flaming buildings to locate an open passage.

Kane headed in the direction where he had seen Samantha behind the buildings. Although it was surprisingly quiet in the back alley, he remained alert as he made his way toward the saloon and the boarding house at the northern-most part of town. The only person he encountered was the sheriff as they glanced at each other from opposite ends of a side alley. They signaled one to the other, and both moved ahead.

The eerie silence was broken by the report of five consecutive shots followed by a single shot several seconds later. Kane's only thought was of Samantha as he broke into a run.

Samantha caught sight of Mississippi as she neared the saloon. He was some distance ahead with three of Crockett's men. It looked as though they were arguing.

252

They had stopped at Pike's insistence, and after a brief conversation the three slipped away down a side alley, while Pike followed the path behind the buildings.

Samantha's heart was beating so intensely she was afraid Pike would hear it. The trembling of her hand made her uncertain as to her ability to hit him from this range if she shot at him. She needed to be closer. Edging herself along as deep in the shadows as she was able, Samantha stalked Pike, praying for a sudden misstep on his part. He passed the block-long saloon which was just beginning to burn and was at the back of the boarding house, one of the few buildings still remaining untouched by the conflagration, when he paused. He leaned over and appeared to be adjusting his boot. Samantha saw her chance. Darting from one shadow to the next, she edged closer and closer to him. He was only ten feet away. She eased the gun up, arms rigid, when suddenly Mississippi whirled around with a sardonic grin on his face. His gun was fixed on her.

"Been lookin' for me, Samantha?" he asked, his voice dripping with sarcasm and hate. "Hope you're luckier than Crockett was."

Samantha jumped back, losing her footing. She caught herself against a wall before she lost her balance entirely. She felt an urge to throw the gun at him and run but fought it, managing to keep her arm rigid, the gun aimed. She began to back up slowly.

"Now where did we leave off?" Mississippi cooed. He took a step toward her. "I can't seem to recall . . ." — another step forward — "where it was . . ." Then he struck in an instant, leaping forward, his arm flashing out. She was in his grip, vise-like on her arm, fingers digging deeply. He pulled her so close she could feel his words on her face as well as hear them as he whispered, "You'll never, never leave me. *Never*. I'd rather see you dead."

Samantha stared at Pike's lips as the words blew out, the spittle collecting about the corners of his mouth. How she hated this man! She moved her gaze up from his lips to his eyes, and in them she saw a craziness. She knew for certain that he *would* kill her, and she drove the gun barrel as hard as she could into his groin. As he doubled over, the air escaping in one great single breath from between his lips, she backed away and bolted for cover.

She was too frightened to run far or fast or even to let out a scream. All she could think of was to find a place to hide. When she made her way around the corner of the boarding house, she saw a group of barrels nestled along the north wall used to store water. She made her way through the maze of the wooden containers and slid down behind one closest to the wall. All she needed, she told herself, was a few minutes to recover her breath and slow down the beating of her heart.

And she was only given minutes. She braced herself against the wall and was ready to push herself up when she heard a plop at the sound of something landing in the barrel near her.

"Samantha!" Mississippi hissed, reminding her of the snake that had taken cover under her skirt in the desert. "S-S-Samantha!"

254

Kane slowed his pace as he approached the rear of the boarding house. He paused before stepping into the open passageway, depending on the strange, flickering, light from the flames cast from overhead to provide him some shimmer of light. The shadows flickered as he crept silently around the corner. A slight movement caused him immediately to withdraw back around the corner where he took cover in the darkened shadow of the building.

It was Pike. And he was alone, making an odd sound. Kane cocked his head, straining to understand what he was saying.

"S-S-Samantha," was what he heard. Samantha was with him! He quickly abandoned the idea of just hauling out and shooting Pike. One of his bullets could find Samantha. He peered around the corner, but it was too dark to make out anything with certainty. As Pike hissed out Samantha's name again, a shot exploded, and then the sound of scuffling feet. Kane steeled himself and started to creep forward as gunshots cracked from the main street to the west of them. Then four more shots.

"Pike, that son of a bitch," Kane hissed.

The flurry of gunfire only served to unnerve Samantha. Her hands began to sweat. Her body shook in a series of convulsive tremors. *I have to get out of here!* she thought. She heard Pike shifting his position.

It was then that Kane fired two shots in the area where he thought Pike to be — in an attempt to draw Pike's attention to him and away from Samantha. He started inching his way forward.

"Give it up, Pike!" Sheriff Brown's voice boomed from somewhere on the other side of the building. "There's nothin' left for you here. Your boys can't back you any more."

Kane felt a wave of relief. "You heard him, Pike," he echoed the sheriff's words. "You're alone." It was then he noticed the roof of the boarding house was aflame.

Pike backed up at the sound of Kane's voice. "I'm not giving up, tin-pan man. Come and get me." Kane had his full attention.

Buoyed by the fact that she was no longer alone, Samantha impulsively jumped up. "Mississippi! You son of a bitch!" she yelled.

"Samantha, stay out of the way!" Kane bellowed as Pike wheeled at the sound of her voice, his gun ready.

Samantha was braced for whatever might happen now. Her gun was clasped in both hands in a steadying grip. Her belly churned, and fear washed over her in waves, but she didn't waver. "You're too much of a coward to shoot me, Mississippi," she stated confidently as she took several steps toward him.

Pike's attention was torn in three directions — toward Samantha, toward Kane, and toward Brown. If he shot Samantha, the next shot would be from Kane's or Brown's gun, and it would be aimed at him. He began stepping backward toward the main street.

"Careful where you step, Pike," Brown cautioned as he engaged himself more closely in the battle.

Panic began to overwhelm Pike as he realized the odds were increasing against him and that none of his men appeared to be anywhere in sight. The realization that his men perhaps *couldn't* come to his aid sent an uncontrollable tremor through his limbs. He stumbled, and, as he did so, he remembered the boarding house had a side door off the kitchen, on this side of the house. As he recovered his footing, he swiveled his body so that he was now backing toward the boarding house and not toward the main street. By glancing quickly to the right in Kane's direction, he could approximate the distance he still had to move.

Kane anticipated Pike's plan and circled away from the building as he moved in on Pike. He tried to get Samantha's attention but could not. He watched as Pike continued to back his way toward what he perceived to be the safety of the building. Kane glanced up and saw that the boarding house's roof was now fully ablaze.

Pike was nearing the doorway.

Then an outlaw, one of Crockett's visitors, a stray the trio had not seen throughout the entire battle, appeared suddenly, rifle in hand, the deadly weapon shifting from Kane to Samantha and back again.

Unsure if the man knew of his presence, Brown raised his gun and shouted: "Put it away, Anderson." Anderson swirled and threw a shot in the direction of Brown's voice. The bullet hit Brown in the upper thigh and sent him spinning to the ground.

Before Kane could respond, Anderson had recovered his previous position, although now his rifle remained stationary, aimed directly at Samantha. Kane braced himself for the shock and then leaped toward

257

Samantha, knocking her clear of the line of fire as he flew through the air.

In the same instant El Diablo appeared out of the darkness. He shouted out Anderson's name and hurled his knife. The outlaw crumbled as he tried to pull the knife out of his belly where it had embedded itself.

"You deserve the horrors of hell, Pike, for what you have done to the woman and the town of Saquarra," El Diablo bellowed.

Pike's gun went off, but the slug went wild as he careened back, crashing into the boarding house's heavy, wooden door. It collapsed into the room beneath his weight. The incoming rush of air fanned the flames that had taken hold of the lower floor, and an instant later Pike was engulfed by those flames.

A rifle coughed loudly close at hand, and a second gun barked its echo.

Kane jerked and stumbled back, a searing, burning sensation ripping a path across his forehead from the left temple. Reason left him in a rush, and he felt himself slipping slowly to the ground. He struggled to right himself as flames spurted from the disintegrating boarding house like they were issuing from the mouth of a volcano. A flaming brand whipped into Samantha's skirts; another swept past her trailing hair; and in a heartbeat the flames rose up around her like a shimmering veil.

Samantha shrieked. Kane tried to rise but couldn't, dizziness washing over him in waves. He heard a voice. "Samantha!" It was his voice. He could not move. "Get down and roll. In the dirt. Do it. Get down!" Kane called.

Samantha could not hear him as she batted ineffectually at the flames and in a panic started to run.

Fighting the sickening waves of blackness, Kane groaned, heaved himself to his knees, and tried to climb to his feet. He could barely make out two figures rolling on the ground as El Diablo, having caught up with Samantha, attempted to smother her burning clothes with his own body. Then all went black.

Kane presently emerged from the darkness. When he came to, El Diablo was at his side. "It is over, my fren'. We have accomplished what you began."

Kane allowed his head to swing back and forth, that effort nearly tumbling him back into unconsciousness. "The price was much too high." He coughed the words out from a throat made raw by smoke. Then he remembered. "Samantha?"

"She ees all right . . . some burns. But, you know, she ees a tough lady." El Diablo shrugged.

"The price was too high," Kane murmured again.

"Who ees to say? The only certainty in Saquarra ees that the people will build again. But with adobe this time."

"Let's get out of here," the peddler said wearily, struggling to his feet. "Fire isn't finished yet." He nodded toward Brown. "Is he okay, too?"

"We are all okay," El Diablo assured him before walking over to Brown and Samantha. El Diablo gently scooped Samantha up in his arms.

The battered foursome, the sheriff limping badly, headed for the south end of town where the people of Saquarra stood watching in numbed silence as the fire burned itself out.

Within minutes Samantha was being cared for by a young Mexican woman, the mother of three children. The children sat quietly at her feet. Despite her wounds, Samantha was entertaining the young ones with rhymes.

The wounds of the other three were bandaged by various townspeople who had formed a sort of makeshift hospital to deal with injuries. With El Diablo's assistance, Kane made his way over to Samantha. As he watched her, slowly a satisfied smile formed on his face.

Samantha glanced up as Brown, a bandage tied around his thigh, limped over to join them.

"They're going to rebuild. Everyone together," Samantha said softly.

"Expected as much," the sheriff returned. "You know, they'll be needing a schoolteacher."

"I'm afraid my reputation wouldn't serve me well on either side of the deadline."

"Who's to say? Crises like these sometimes have a way of evening everybody out, giving everybody a new start."

"Memory is one thing that a fire can't destroy, Sheriff," Samantha stated flatly. "I expect memories are about the only thing the people of Saquarra will have left a couple days from now. No, I just can't see how I'd fit in any better than I have up until now."

Kane, listening to the conversation, stood quietly, studying what remained of Saquarra. The fire had burned itself out. All that remained were softly glowing coals and the dawn, painting the sky soft hues of pink in the east. The destruction had been total. Nothing had been spared, save the adobe walls and, ironically, his peddler's wagon and that only by virtue of the fact the wind had been blowing in the wrong direction to carry the flames to it.

"I'm tired," Kane admitted to no one in particular, "but I used to be a mighty good hand at building. I might even be convinced to do it again." Then he directed his words to Samantha. "I'll give you a ride out of here when we're through rebuilding if you still have a mind to go."

"I'd like that . . . thank you."

El Diablo smiled, and it was not one of deprecation or superiority. "It would be interesting to begin again. It would be interesting, too, to see the wolf domesticated, eh, El Lobo?" He passed a meaningful glance in Samantha's direction.

Kane gave him a strange half smile, quirking the corners of his lips.

"The name's Kane, Zachariah Kane."

El Diablo grinned with the knowing look of a philosopher. "And I am Descanso Cordova." He thrust out his hand and gripped Kane's in a firm shake.

About Author

P(eggy) A(nne) Bechko was born in South Haven, Michigan. She had always loved the American West and, when young, visited it frequently. She wrote her first Western novel, *The Night of the Flaming Guns* (1974), at the age of twenty-two. She signed the manuscript P. A. Bechko, so it came as a surprise when her agent, who had never before spoken to her, telephoned to say that Doubleday had made an offer on it. Her editor at Doubleday was no less surprised when he saw her full legal name. In 1981 Bechko finally moved to where she wanted most to be, Santa Fé, New Mexico. Together with her mother and with occasional help from her brother, she went about completing from the ground up much of the home in which she now lives. She married a fellow writer in 1995. In addition to two original paperback Westerns, Bechko also branched out in the 1980s to write romance novels for Harlequin, but with authentic Western settings, such as her historical romance, *Cloud Dancer* (1991). Her books, beginning with her Western novels, have been translated into the principal European languages, including French, German, Italian, Spanish, and

Dutch. Virtually all of her Western stories have appeared in large print editions and some in audio editions. The late C. L. Sonnichsen writing in *El Paso Times* described Bechko as "one of the few women in the business, but she outdoes many of her male counterparts in fertility of imagination."